JAMIE'S ADVENTURES IN TIME
FINDING HUGH MILLER

BY LESLEY BEAKE

DEDICATION

For my mother, Sheila and to the fine people in Scotland who welcomed me back as if I had never been away.
Thank you.

NOTE ON THIS STORY:

Hugh Miller, writer, geologist, stonemason and thinker, lived in Scotland all his life (1802-1856). He was Scottish to the very core of his being and he wrote wonderful prose describing both the landscape and a way of life that was changing forever. He is remembered with great affection for his way with words, his way of looking at the world and his intense observation of everything he saw around him. He didn't just look — he looked and then thought. Then he wrote down what was in his mind in a way that remains clear and eloquent today, even if the sentences, and often the words, are longer than we are used to in a world of sound bites and text messages. He was famous in his own place and his own time, and known around the world for his discoveries of fossils and his writing about deep time and the landscape. Why is he still famous? Maybe because he left something behind that allows us a glimpse of what it was like to be Hugh Miller. Perhaps that was what caught, and held, the attention of young Jamie Alexander two centuries later when he accidentally found himself deep in Hugh's world; deep in his mind.

First published in Great Britain in 2012 by
For The Right Reasons
Printers & Publishers
60 Grant Street, Inverness, IV3 8BS
and
Henry McKenzie Johnston

ISBN: 978-1-905787-61-6

CHAPTER ONE

I have been sent to the end of the world. I knew it when the familiar English names began to slip away behind me on the railway tracks and we crossed a border to somewhere else. I knew it when we passed a city in the south sometime in the night, and when the train slid into Inverness, cold and dark and wet in the early morning. I knew it when my grandfather's face appeared — unsmiling — at the carriage window and he looked, for a moment, into my eyes. I knew it. Then there was another journey, in his rattling old car, to a place with a hard name. The Black Isle. Not as black as my heart.

Scotland. Mum says I came here once when I was little. I don't remember. I don't remember the drive north or the long bridge stretching ahead into the soggy mist or the fields of yellow stuff glowing beside the road. Some shaggy cows blundered across it and then vanished into the white. A man in a cap waved at my grandfather and the sweep, sweep of the windscreen wipers went on and then on. I had forgotten the little cottages along the way and the sheep with their lambs looking at us as we passed. And then the slowing of the old car and the crowding of grey-stone buildings, windows painted soft blues and greens; the cry of seagulls down at the harbour... and we had arrived. Here we were in the small town of Cromarty on the Black Isle in the Highlands of Scotland - more like a village than a town after

London: Cromarty, to where I have been sent in my disgrace and as my punishment.

I only remembered my grandfather's house when he unlocked the door of the cottage and swung it open. It smelled of cabbage, just as it did when I came here before. Can things get worse?

Well they can of course, and they did. My grandfather took only a few short days to snap, less than a week. My 'insolence' he said it was, but I said nothing. Maybe that was it; the saying no words, the smiling no smiles. So now I am here, locked up in a half-empty cottage across the road from his house with a candle and some matches for when it gets dark, and the rain still sliding down the windows, and my heart still black.

'You need to cool off, James Alexander,' my grandfather said. Cool *off*? In this temperature? It was supposed to be spring, but in this place it felt more like winter. 'You need time for reflection,' he said, sticking a horrible old red book and a notebook and pen down on the desk in front of me. 'You need to reflect on how lucky you are,' he said. 'You need to think about things,' he said. And then I heard the click of the lock on the door and the sound of his footsteps. Damn!

Well, I did the usual stuff. Swore. Banged on the door. Tried the windows — screwed shut. Swore some more. Nobody came.

After a while I decided to save my energy, for survival. It was getting even colder, something I had not thought possible. It was also getting dark. I swore some more. It didn't help. I looked around.

My grandfather had clearly been planning this. There was a candle and some matches. There was a blanket. There was even a packet of biscuits. (Stale). I ate the biscuits and drank some water from the tap in the kitchen. I thought about a Big Mac and some Coke. I swore some more.

It was very boring in the stupid cottage and it was getting dark. I lit the candle. I put the blanket round me. It was a very *quiet* kind of cold. There were no streetlights shining in, no sounds of traffic, no sirens in the distance and no music. I missed music. My grandfather's house didn't have any, just clocks ticking and then gonging on when one of them reached some or other hour. I felt my anger again, like hot lava from a volcano. How long had I been angry? I couldn't remember. I couldn't remember *not* being angry, angry and sad.

The chair was hard. Something white flapped past the dark window. A big moth? Or what?

The shapes of the windows were dark purple. Soon it would be really, really dark. People would be able to see in the windows, be able to see me sitting here with my one blazing candle. For a moment I remembered how Georgie Crawford and I used to go round the estate looking in the windows to see if we could see anything interesting, like girls undressing or anything. We never did, but it was a laugh. I wished Georgie Crawford was still … here.

I tried the door again, just in case, and the windows. Nothing budged. I suppose they were made to keep out hundred-mile an hour winds and six-foot snow drifts. There was nothing else to do, so I sat on the chair again and swore a bit more. Swearing helps, but not if there is nobody to get shocked and tick you off and go red in the face and tell you about modern boys and how they don't know how lucky they are. Yeah, right, lucky.

I thought I might as well look at the book. There was nothing else to do. It was called *My Schools and Schoolmasters: or, the story of my education* and it was by somebody called Hugh Miller. Catchy title, I *don't* think. It was probably boring. I just flipped it open … and there it was, a ghost story, just what I didn't need. But it was a good story. What Miss Edgar would call: 'An excellent piece of narrative description.' And then she would get one of the bright-boys to read it aloud — and that wouldn't be me. But it *was* good.

It was Jack's story and the writer, this Hugh Miller, said he had heard it told many times when he was a child, because it was a story about his own father, who was the master of a ship. Maybe he felt as if he had really been there — like I did. Because, when I started reading, it was as if ... as if I was there on the deck of the ship half-laden with coal and there was a massive storm on, and it was dark as could be, and it was two hundred years ago off this freezing Scottish coast, not all that far from where I was sitting now:

Jack was on the ship and they were just about to leave the shelter of the harbour at Peterhead when a young woman appeared at the side of the boat with a small child in her arms pleading with young Hugh's father to take her on board. She was a soldier's wife, on her way to her husband at Fort George, she said, but she had run out of funds and had nowhere to sleep. Would they take her?

Jack waited for the master to say no. It was foolish to take a woman on board with a storm coming, and a sick woman at that from the looks of things. But the master just thought for a moment and then his mouth softened and he showed her to come on board — and Jack knew right then that it was bad, bad, bad.

The woman took the child down below and the master closed her in safe and sure but hardly had the ship left port than the wind came on. Not just a wind but a hurricane, Jack says, and blowing snow for all it was worth.

The master and his crew fought that wind with everything they knew, but the load of coal they carried was shifting in the hull below their feet and there was danger everywhere. The lantern threw just enough light over the master's face to show how worried he was as he steered the ship, but Jack was looking at something else, something that made him cold with fear. Beside the master — now on one side, now on the other — was the woman and her child.

How could the master be so foolish? It was sheer madness to let them on deck in such a storm! But when Jack went to say something, the master turned his blue eyes on him calmly. 'What woman? What child?' he asked, looking around. Jack could see them as plain as plain, but the master could not. And then they were gone — and the evidence of the hatch, close closed and locked from the outside, said they were safe below.

Jack had no time to think more about this mystery, because the storm came full at them then. 'I have never seen a ship live in as bad a night as this,' the master told Jack and they set about trying to save her.

For a moment, I looked around at the cottage. I felt as if I had come home from the storm myself. Hugh Miller had made the ship and the decks of her rolling with the wind so real in my mind. I thought I could hear the sound of the storm howling like a thousand devils through the rigging and feel the fear of the crew. I didn't want to read more, but I did. I couldn't stop:

Blue light glimmered on the wet deck and when Jack and the master looked up at the mast, slow, cold dead-fire hung in the crosstrees of the rigging. 'It's all over with us now!' Jack cried. But the master was calm. 'Nay man,' he said, steady as anything. 'If you can keep us safe from the shifting coal, I'll be your guarantee against the deadlight. It's only natural — like lightning.'

But Jack knew better. After a long night fighting the storm, the ship was struck by a heavy wave and the coal shifted one last time in the hold. There was no steering her and she floundered along the coast until at daybreak she struck the terrible bar of Findhorn and the surf came rolling over, half a mast high. The master bravely fought the wave to get the hatch open and the woman and child out, but he was washed away from them and they, poor things, were drowned. The master and the crew saw the bodies later, floating out of the side of the ship where a wave had broken her, the child still clutched in the woman's arms.

That ship was called *The Friendship*.

I don't know how long I sat there, the candle guttering in the draught from under the back door, the book still open in front of me. But I jumped about a mile high when a hand came down hard on my shoulder, and I probably shrieked like a girl as well for all I know.

'Aye,' said my grandfather's voice from behind. 'That was one of my favourite stories of that book when I was a lad.' Then, because old people can never resist it, he gave me a short speech. This one was about how the captain of the ship had been Hugh Miller's father and how he had saved himself from that wreck — but been drowned when his next ship went down soon afterwards. Then, while the candle gave the last of its light, he made a longer speech about how Hugh Miller was one of Scotland's greatest sons and a lot of other stuff I stopped listening to after the bit about him becoming a stonemason when he left school. What for? Who would want to travel around working on cold, hard stones all the time?

Finally, he wound up talking about Hugh Miller, the greatest, or maybe second-greatest son of Scotland, and suggested we go and have soup.

'You could have switched the electric light on,' he remarked, pointing to a switch I hadn't noticed. 'And there's a bar heater over there you could have used as well.'

Rats! But I had the sense to keep my swearing inside my head as I followed him across the street to his own cottage.

CHAPTER TWO

'Aye,' my grandfather said again after he had locked up, stepping quickly across the cold street and into his nearly as chilly home. 'I was always fond of *Schools and Schoolmasters*,' and he nodded towards the book. 'It spoke to me, it did. I could imagine I was really in the story, not just reading it.'

I watched his hands as he opened a can of Heinz tomato soup, big strong hands like my grandfather himself. We always have Heinz tomato soup. I don't think he knows that Heinz make any other kinds. I didn't say anything about the book. He would tell me anyway.

My grandfather, after a short pause, obliged. 'He built another ship, Hugh Miller's father did. He was not a man to give up easily, no, not him! He lost a lot, but he kept on going. He had just built a house, quite a grand one, but he lived in the cottage next door with his wife and three bairns. The cottage and the house are just up the street … museums now …' Lost in thought, my grandfather paused, remembering, as if *he* had been there with Hugh Miller's father. 'He built a new ship — a sloop with two white stripes along the sides. You could see the square topsails clear as clear when she came into port and young Hugh used to go and watch for her coming.'

My grandfather's hands went on making preparations and I watched him pour the soup into a battered old saucepan and put it on the stove. His hands trembled, I noticed, for all his strength. He was getting old.

'Funny thing, though, when young Hugh's father really *was* lost at sea — when young Hugh was maybe five years of age — the lad saw the ghost of the woman that drowned with her child. The one you were reading about when I near frightened you half to death.' I didn't say anything. I had *not* been frightened, well, not much.

My grandfather was enjoying the story. 'He only saw her arm

and her hand — still dripping with the sea, and just at the time when his poor father was drowned in that same water, just at that time. The door blew open and he was sent to shut it. And there was the arm … just there, with sea water dripping and nothing where the body should have been.' My grandfather nodded. 'The servant girl saw it too,' he added, as if that put the lid on that.

I didn't say anything. But a cold, drowned finger seemed to touch the back of my neck and I shivered in spite of the feeble fire he had lit.

We had our soup — *slurped* our soup — and ate the last of an elderly loaf of bread ('waste not, want not,' my grandfather remarked with some satisfaction).

'When I was your age …' it was my grandfather again. I thought I was in for yet another lecture but no, this time he was back on the book. '… I used to read all the time.' He nodded towards the bookcase. There was a whole row of old red books, just like *Schools and Schoolmasters*! It was a damn *series*! 'You should read more. You would do well to start with a good book like this one.' He stroked the cover. Then he laughed suddenly, startling me. 'You'd like it! He ran away from school, Hugh Miller did.' He looked at me sideways, a bit sly. 'After getting into a fight with his schoolmaster.'

That *did* get my interest. A sudden vision of Mr Maggs, great, bullying Maths-Maggs lying on the floor with me standing over him, triumphant, flashed through my mind — and then flashed out again. Mr Maggs was much too big for me. But I felt a little bit … well, interested in this Hugh Miller.

'Aye …' grandfather was back in the conversation … 'there's a lot to learn in that book.' He touched it again, gently. 'Maybe I'll read a bit to you.' There was a kind of question in his voice. It wasn't his usual statement of fact. My grandfather's speech didn't normally do much punctuation.

I thought about it. My grandfather didn't own a television. My i-Pod and my mobile had been confiscated after the … well, before I left home. At least it would give him something to do. 'Sure,' I said, not looking up. So he did.

First he got me to bank up the fire, while he ran the tap over the tomato–soup–stained plates and spoons and put the saucepan in soak. He always puts the pan in soak. The soup usually catches just a bit before he remembers about it. Then he got his glasses and settled himself. I sat in the opposite chair — the one my grandmother used to sit in. I think he misses her. He never talks about her, but sometimes there are small pauses in the conversation and when that happens, he always looks across at this chair … as if he was *thinking* about her.

He glanced at the fire. I'd taken the chance and put more coal on than we usually got. 'Humph! That will keep us going until next winter!' He found his place, cleared his throat for about ten minutes, and began. I knew it was another of his favourite bits because he went straight for it.

I was thinking that maybe I could make money by recording all this stuff and selling it to people who couldn't get to sleep at night, when suddenly I found that I was really listening. Hugh Miller certainly knew how to tell a good story. The pictures he had seen with *his* eyes were in my mind now too.

Scotland. I began to see another Scotland, one that was not a prison for boys who behaved badly (like me) but a place where that boy might run free and have ... I suppose I was thinking that he might have fun. I expected Hugh Miller to be the kind of boy grandfathers approve of; the kind who does well at school and behaves properly and does the right thing at all times ... but he wasn't.

He wrote in a very stiff way, with long sentences and sometimes I had to listen really carefully to understand what he meant. But he was writing about a place that had changed and a time that was over two hundred years ago. It must have been a lot different being a boy then, a *lot* different. This is what Hugh sounds like:

'I was born in the town of Cromarty on 10th October 1802. My father, whom I can barely remember, was master and owner of a small trading sloop. Towards the close of the year 1807 he left Cromarty on a voyage to the western Highlands for a cargo of kelp, and on his return his vessel was driven by stress of weather into Peterhead. From that port he wrote my mother the last letter she ever received from him; for on the day he sailed from it there arose a terrible storm in which many seamen perished and he was never heard of again.'

I went on listening, but my mind was thinking at the same time about what that would be like for a little boy of five years old to know that his father had drowned. I thought about Hugh Miller, down at the seashore, or up on a hill behind his mother's house where he sometimes used to keep watch, straining his eyes for sight of the sloop with the two white painted lines that would whisper that his father had come home to him after all. He would remember Jack's story. He would be able to see the ship in the storm and the breaking of her in the cold, cold, night sea. I closed my heart to what he must have felt although I thought I knew.

Dad left when I was about the same age. I didn't go down to the harbour, or even to the end of the road, looking out for him like Hugh did. I was glad to see Dad go, after what he did. But the effect on me, and Mum, was about the same. She had no way to pay the bills unless she went out to work. Mum went back to her job in marketing — and she was good. She got better and better jobs and travelled a lot, but she had to keep at it. She works very hard, but I miss her sometimes, and the way we used to be before Dad left. I stayed home, sometimes with my dad's mum, until she died. I think she preferred Mum to her own son. She certainly never had a good word to say for him.

Hugh's mother took in needlework. I asked my grandfather what that actually meant. He stopped reading and looked at me for a moment, quite shocked. 'Mending and making clothes,' he said after a pause, 'for people who were rich enough to pay. In those days people didn't just go to chain stores and buy new things. They made and mended.' I tried to imagine Mum doing that, and failed.

Hugh Miller had two uncles though, something I don't have, and they taught him things they thought he should know — not like school, but really interesting things; what kind of fish to catch and how to catch them, and the names of the small creatures on the hill and how to recognise a bird by its song when he couldn't see it. Stuff like that.

My grandfather's voice went steadily on. The fire brightened and then faded to a red glow, warming the room; keeping out the dark. My mind was out on the summer hills with young Hugh and I was breathing the scent of freedom. That's where I wanted to be, outside. I wanted to be free.

There seemed always to be sunshine and when it did rain a bit, young Hugh never cared, but searched the woods and streams and hillsides for things that interested him, bringing them home to show his uncles and find out what they were. He found trees turned into something other than wood, so long had they been there, and hazelnuts turned into stone. There was a place with a lovely name — The Moss of the Willows — somewhere I longed to explore myself. Here, in some swampy ground young Hugh dug out of the mud a flat piece of horn that looked like nothing he had seen before. His Uncle James looked at it very carefully when it was presented to him.

'That is the horn,' Uncle James said after a while, 'of no deer that now lives in this country. We have the red deer and the fallow deer and the roe, and none of them have horns at all like that. I never saw an elk, but I am pretty sure this broad, plank-like horn can be none other than the horn of an elk.' And they took it to some people who were working nearby and everyone examined it, and a man who was there as a customer had a look at it too.

'That horn,' the customer said solemnly, 'has lain in the Moss of the Willows for perhaps half a century.'

'Half a century, sir!' Uncle James shouted. 'Half a *century*! Was the elk a native of Scotland half a century ago? There is no notice of the elk, sir, in British history. That horn must have lain in the Moss of the Willows for *thousands* of years!'

My grandfather enjoyed that, taking the part of Uncle James as if he had known him personally and emphasising the good bits. 'So was it a fossil?' I asked.

My grandfather looked at me as if he wondered whether I was ready for the answer. 'It was,' he said at last. 'It was the beginning of Hugh Miller's interest in geology.'
'I thought you said he was a stonemason!'
'I did. He was.'
'But ...'

My grandfather went calmly on. 'He was a self-made man, in the days when that was just possible. He rejected a formal education — college and so forth — and chose instead to educate himself by reading and listening. And his first work was as a stonemason — when he was not a great deal older than you are now — travelling around Scotland wherever there was need of his skill. It was a hard life.'

I thought a bit. 'So … did he find fossils in the places where he cut stone?'

'Nearby,' my grandfather said. 'Good building stone doesn't usually have fossils. But he noticed other things that made him wonder — like water ripples in solid rock. And when people saw his interest, they told him about other unusual things. Hugh had the ability to listen. And then to want find out about what he had heard — and of course he had the skill with the hammer. For the stones,' he added kindly.

'And did people know much about fossils in those days?
My grandfather hesitated, as if we were swimming into deeper waters than he cared for just yet.

'No. There was a lot of talk about what was being discovered — what was being *noticed* — but Geology was a new science. In fact it wasn't even a science yet. People were … theorizing. It was a time of great change in the way people thought about the world'

'And are fossils geology?'
My grandfather shot me a look to see if I was really asking, or trying to be funny. I was really asking. 'Well …' He thought for a bit. 'Fossils are like markers in the stone that help geologists unravel the history of life on Earth.' He looked at me again, more

kindly. 'People didn't specialize as much in those days.'

Something occurred to me. I sat up straight. 'When was Hugh Miller born?' I asked. My grandfather gave me one of his sidelong looks. 'Didn't I say? He was born in 1802.'

I was thinking. 'And when did Charles Darwin publish his book on evolution?' My grandfather didn't approve. He could see where I was going. '1859,' he said shortly.

'So …' I began, but my grandfather cut me short.
'Make no assumptions, laddie,' he said, closing the book with a snap. 'Make no assumptions.' He looked at one of the clocks — the one that is fast. 'And it's time for your bed.'

CHAPTER THREE

I went to bed even if it was only ten to ten (by some clocks). You don't argue with my grandfather. Anyway, I didn't feel all that good. My head hurt and my throat was sore. So I took two of the aspirins Mum had packed in my sponge bag and got into my damp and freezing bed.

I thought I would sleep, but I didn't. I seemed to be dreaming all night. Some of the dreams were good ones. I drifted among ferny forests and the sun shone low through tall, dark trees. Clouds of midges spiralled up in the light and there was soft, springy grass under my feet. Everything in my dream seemed to be stronger and better than it was in real life. I took my shoes and socks off and paddled in a brown river with patterns on it like tortoise shells and I laughed so that my laughter went up into the sky that was high above the tall trees.

Some of the dreams were nightmares. I saw the arm and the hand of the woman who drowned and it went before me wherever I looked and wherever I walked so that my feet stumbled and I fell, and the mud where I landed was soft and swallowed me up. I knew I would be trapped in that mud for thousands of years, thousands. I was a small boy, so small that I could hardly be seen with a telescope from a ship that was drowning in saltwater waves. The cries of the sailors filled my ears and it was cold ... cold, cold.

Far away, I heard a voice I knew. It was my grandfather. I opened my eyes — and then shut them quickly.

'Why are you still in bed?' he asked in that crusty way he has. Then he must have had a better look at me because next thing I felt his hand on my forehead, testing my temperature. It was the first time he had touched me since he had collected me at the station a week before.

'Sick, hey?' He sounded doubtful, as if I might just be pretending, but worried too. Then I drifted away again, in a lifeboat that was full with too many men and a wind that roared and thundered against sharp grey cliffs and rocks that could smash a man, or a boat — or a boy — in seconds.

It got worse. Once, when I tried to open my eyes, there was a *girl* sitting in the room. She was all shining and silvery against the light of the window. I thought she might be a ghost ... but she looked as if she was doing homework — which was horrible, because it made the dream seem more ... possible somehow. Surely ghosts don't have homework? She spoke. 'Are you feeling any better?' I went back to the other dreams.

My throat was on fire and my head hurt more than I could have believed possible. Another voice came — a woman — I wondered if she was a doctor. There was the cold of a stethoscope on my chest (why can't they just warm them up a bit?) rumblings of talk between her and my grandfather. I caught the words, 'lot of it about,' and 'extremely bad strain, this year. I'll write you a note for his school. I'll have to warn you that he will need plenty of rest, quiet and time to get over this.' I gathered I had some horrible virus, but that I would live — maybe — and be OK in a week or so, probably. I drifted off again.

Somebody brought lemon barley water. I knew what it was because I'd had it when I was little. My other grandmother, my dad's mum, gave it to me to drink when I had my tonsils out. But I knew I was still sick and dreaming because the ghost-girl was still there. 'Do you want me to read to you?' it asked. 'Your grandfather said I should. He said you like that.' Maybe I nodded. It started reading anyway. Hugh Miller, of course. What else could I expect? What happened to Walter Scott and that poetry guy who wrote about the wee cowering beastie? Robert Burns .. and all those other Scottish writers? Yeah. What happened to them? I thought of the Hugh Miller Series stretching out along the bookshelf. I had better get better — quick.

I let my eyes open just a little bit, so she couldn't see I was looking. She was very small and very thin. She would break, I thought, if a strong wind blew on her. Her very light hair was even lighter when the sun shone suddenly through the window behind her head. When she raised her eyes and looked straight at me (she knew I was watching her) her eyes were a strange kind of silver like … almost like moonlight. I shut my eyes again, tightly.

The words came pouring past me like sea currents cutting through the ocean and making for somewhere that was, in this case, my brain. There was nothing to do but listen. Sometimes the ghost-girl read, and sometimes my grandfather did — and sometimes there was just cool and lovely silence that floated above the ocean currents of words and pleased me.

His uncles introduced young Hugh to stories — stories first and then books. My grandfather liked that bit a lot. I could hear that when he read. He was putting special effects in, like different voices. Young Hugh felt exactly the same about school as I did. His first little school was OK — dame's school, they called it then — but when he got into big school, things took a turn for the worse. He wrote about how he wondered what on earth he was learning for. What was the point of it all? And then he discovered that the point of it was *books* — and the way he could discover stories for himself was by reading. I supposed that was before you got them from television. I smiled, inside my mind, at the idea of sharing that idea with my grandfather.

Young Hugh read his way through all his uncles' books, and all the books that were there to be read in those days in a busy fishing and trading town. Cromarty was a big item in the coastal trade in those days, my grandfather told me. Captains of ships and their crewmen, traders and soldiers, anyone who could read, brought books back in their baggage and they were carefully kept in the cottages of those who loved such things. Books were *important* in Scotland, my grandfather said (like they weren't in England, I supposed). Hugh read and he read and read. He kept the books he was given in a little wooden box made of birch-bark. I liked to think of him taking his books out and looking at the pictures some of them had and then putting them back in his little birch-bark box.

He read some books I had heard of — like *Robinson Crusoe* and

Gulliver's Travels — and some I had seen films of, but none I had actually read. If I had been properly awake I was sure my grandfather would have asked me, fixing me with his sharp blue eyes and looking disappointed when I said I had not. 'Missed an experience you'll regret later!' he might well have said, ploughing on with *Schools and Schoolmasters*.

They read aloud in Hugh's time too. He makes a word-picture of his Uncle James, the saddler, working on saddles and harnesses in the evenings at the kitchen table by candlelight while his brother Sandy read aloud and neighbours sometimes dropped in too. ' … the book,' Hugh says, 'would sometimes be laid aside in order that its contents might be discussed in conversation.' For a moment a picture of switching off the telly at home for discussion of the programmes (even during the adverts) popped into my mind — and then popped out again. But I loved it when young Hugh said this about his uncle:

> 'There are professors of natural history who knew less about living nature than was known by my uncle Sandy.'

The man and the boy used to walk together often after work finished for the day, watching out for interesting things like lobsters casting sets of legs and claws when they got a fright. Uncle Sandy told Hugh that once, when he fired a musket over a pool where a lobster was hiding, it cast off both its great claws without even a thought for the future, just as frightened soldiers would throw away their weapons. I wish I had been there to see that. I wish I had an uncle, one who would even *think* of firing muskets over lobsters.

It wasn't proper school, Hugh says, and he had no need to play truant from this kind of learning, but he paid tribute — often — to how much he had learned from his uncles in this other kind of school.

Young Hugh was a wild little boy, always up on the hills, or along the seashore, playing … and also looking, always looking at things and always curious. He wanted to go to sea at first, like his father and grandfather before him, and *his* father too. But, as they had all — every one of them — been lost at sea, his mother must have been quite glad when he changed his mind.

It was a book, of course, that did it, a book his uncle introduced him to about the Scottish hero William Wallace. At first young Hugh didn't want to read it (it wasn't about sailors and sea battles) but it lay about for so long that eventually he did read a bit, and his uncle encouraged him to read more. Now he had something to think about other than just the sea. He began to realise that he lived in a bigger place than Cromarty, with its fine sea harbour and many ships. He began to get the feeling that became a great love of his life — the feeling of Scotland.

Now he wandered along the seashore and on the hills making up enormous long verses for himself — verses that nobody else could share, because he couldn't write yet. Thank heavens. Otherwise there would have been even more pages of *Schools and Schoolmasters* — and I don't like poetry.

They made young Hugh go to school, of course. Scotland has always been big on schools. He wasn't very good at being at school. In fact, he was pretty bad at it. He didn't pay attention at all and he skipped it altogether when he thought he could get away with it. My grandfather made a long speech about that between chapters one morning when I was starting to feel a bit better, at last. 'Hugh Miller was no … what you might call *example* when he was young,' my grandfather admitted. 'He was …well, he was a bit of a …'

'Dropout,' I was thinking in my brain. But that wasn't the word my grandfather came up with. '…*individual*,' he managed at last. 'An individual!'

There was a quiet space where I just floated like a piece of seaweed on a quiet tide, in and out, in and out. I could hear the sound of small waves somewhere behind me, somewhere near my grandfather's house, and I knew the sea was real. I curled my toes, imagining how cold the water would be.

The trees outside were beginning to green. I could almost see the buds unfolding in the first real spring sunshine and a scent of flowers came in at the window. There was some kind of statue up the hill on a tall column. There were always birds sitting on its head. I'd try opening my eyes suddenly to catch them out, but there was always one.

'That's Hugh Miller,' my grandfather said suddenly one day into a silence. 'Up there.'
'What!'
For once, he let my bad manners pass. 'Aye,' he went on, 'that statue up there on the pillar. Hugh Miller.'
I couldn't think of anything to say.
'Hugh Miller,' he went on relentlessly, 'the famous geologist and newspaper editor.'

I didn't want to know about that. I didn't want my friend Hugh to be a famous person, an adult, a newspaper editor (how did he get to be that?). I wanted him to stay a boy like me, learning and teaching himself interesting things. I wanted … I wanted us both to stay boys, stay boys and stay in the happy time that was Hugh Miller's childhood in the woods and on the beaches of Cromarty, two hundred years in the past.

I must have dozed off then, because the girl-ghost was reading when I next swam up to the surface of my dreams. She had a nicer voice than my grandfather — although I noticed that she also liked to act up the interesting bits. Her eyes were more blue today than silver. It must have been a trick of the light when I first looked, but her hair was still pale gold. She had brushed it recently. You could still see the brush-marks on it. It wasn't difficult to look at the ghost girl — but I made sure she didn't see me doing it.

Hugh's life was an interesting one. He explored, sometimes on his own and sometimes with his uncles, and sometimes with some other boys. I listened quite hard to those parts. I've never had a gang — never even been in one. There was just the feeling of one, sometimes, with Georgie Crawford, when we were little. Even when the two of us were together, we always stayed, or were pushed, outside the big circle where the main boys were.

It sounded as if Hugh Miller didn't always fit in either. Sometimes he played on his own on the beach, making things he'd read about. He knew the other boys laughed at him, but he didn't care. I followed him in my mind, with my eyes closed, and watched him.

Other times he was the leader of the gang because his books told him about things the other boys didn't know — battle plans and how to build forts, stuff like that. But I think he was happy on his own too. He always seemed to be busy with something — or reading, or thinking about it.

I sometimes think about the big things — the things you can't miss, like mountains and islands and huge clouds piled up on the edge of the sky when there's going to be a storm, that sort of thing. But young Hugh got down on his knees and looked at the very small things growing on the rocks, he looked under the water at what was going on there and he looked behind things and on top of things and went into places where it probably wasn't safe for small boys to go on their own.

I don't really *look* at things — mostly because it gets scary when you think too much. It's easier to turn down the contrast, like you can do on a television, so that it's not so black and white, but kind of grey and safe. When I listened to young Hugh's voice in his book, I could hear that he never did that. When he went for a walk, he experienced everything, from tiny lichens growing on a rock to great cliffs that had broken with the pounding of the sea, giving up their secrets. He watched. He listened. And, the more I heard him, through his words in a book read by an old man and a ghost girl, the more I knew that he *cared*.

I wondered if I would ever be brave enough to care again.

CHAPTER FOUR

I took a long time to get better. I didn't really mind. It was quiet and restful in the narrow bed up under the roof in the attic room. Hugh Miller was with me, sometimes even when I was asleep. The ghost girl — she wasn't a ghost, her name was Alice and she lived next door — came every day after school and continued reading to me from where they had left off the day before. When it was his turn to read, my grandfather thundered away as if he was auditioning for a part in a radio play. Neither of them seemed to mind, or notice, when I dropped off. They just kept right on with *Schools and Schoolmasters* as if it was their duty to get through it before I could escape.

The bit my grandfather enjoyed most was young Hugh at school. Wow! I wish I'd gone to that one! They had a pig-slaughtering place next door — well, close by where the boys got practical experience in animal anatomy. They had fighting-cock competitions, although young Hugh never took part in them, just paying his sixpence subscription a year and pretending he had one. I have no idea what a cockfight might have been like — and I don't want to imagine — but a *school* having one!

The school was a long, low building, open at both ends, with a hard-packed mud floor and a thatched roof above. The windows of the school looked out over the sea and the boys could see when the boats came in — and watch when they were supposed to be attending to their lessons

'There was perhaps no educational institution in the kingdom in which all sorts of barques and carvels, from the fishing yawl to the frigate, could be more correctly drawn on the slate, or where any defect in hulk or rigging, in some faulty delineation, was sure of being more justly and unsparingly criticised.'

In other words, the boys did a lot of looking out of the window. Hugh-speak is quite complicated, but I was beginning to get the hang of it. He sure did enjoy words!

When the herring boats came in, the boys could tell, from how deep they were in the water, how good the catch had been. If there were too many fish to be dealt with by salting and curing, a pile of silvery fish would be left at the schoolhouse door and a crowd of people would arrive to haggle over the catch.

Best of all was when the peat boats came in with fuel for the people's fires. They were supposed to give peats to the school, to keep the children warm in their classroom on the freezing mornings. It was a local law. But sometimes the crew tried to get away with it and the schoolmaster would let the boys go and 'borrow' something off the boat until the sailors gave in and 'bought' it back with the peats they should have given in the first place.

I lay there, quite still in my bed, and could see through Hugh's eyes. The cold morning when the freezing wet mist hugged the shore and the peat fire in the draughty classroom smoked so that they could hardly read the letters on their slates. Then the sudden release — and the gang of boys sneaking onto the boats to take a boathook or an oar and then dashing off with it. I *wished* I could have been part of that!

Young Hugh was busy being an individual most of the time and not paying any attention to his lessons. He used to tell the other boys stories in class and the schoolmaster didn't seem to care whether anybody was listening to *him* or not. He taught the ones that wanted to be taught and let the others do what they wanted.

At first young Hugh used to tell the stories that he had read in books, but when he ran out of these, he started to make up his own — sometimes just using bits of the stories in the books. The other boys called him 'Sennachie'. My grandfather told me that means 'storyteller' in Gaelic, or something like it. Gaelic is very complicated.

Being a sennachie must have been good practice for Hugh Miller later when he had to write about a million pages of *Schools and*

Schoolmasters and the rest of his series. I wondered, if I was sick for a year, would we get through it? Even with two readers going at it hammer and tongs whenever I was awake?

I got to like young Hugh more and more. And then came the best bit. The ghost-girl was reading when I woke up and boy, was she exercised about this part of Hugh's story!

They were big on spelling in those days. Everybody had to spell out the words in a special way, separating the syllables. The ghost-girl had quite a lot to say about that. She did a little act of spelling things out and being the teacher. I tried opening my eyes, but the light hurt too much, so I closed them again.

'Spell 'awful', she demanded, being the teacher.
Then she was Hugh Miller. 'a-w-f-u-l.'
'No!' she said, using a schoolteacher voice that was *just* like Mr Maggs
Hugh Miller's voice did it again. 'a-w-f-u-l.'
The ghost-girl made a sudden smacking noise with something and I jumped in my bed. 'No! It must be spelled like this — a-w, aw, f-u-l, awful.'

Young Hugh didn't see the sense in this, and neither did I. It sounded like one of those theories that teachers sometimes invent to make children miserable. There were more smacking noises from the ghost-girl. Young Hugh was being beaten by the master for his cheek. Again and again came the smacking noises! And then she read on about how the schoolmaster became so angry that he wrestled with Hugh, throwing him down to the floor in a temper.

They swayed from side to side of the school room, now backwards, now forwards, for a full minute before Hugh tripped over something - and the school master was immediately upon him, beating him so hard that the boy was filled with aches and bruises for a month afterwards.

When it was over, young Hugh took his hat from the hat peg in the corner of the room and left the school - forever.

Hurrah! *Go, Hugh! Go, Hugh!*

My mind wanted to think about how *I* had left school — and hoped it was forever, but I didn't let it. I didn't want to be back there in Canon Hills Comprehensive with the smell of school dinners and school toilets and the sneering of Malcolm Todd … and the rest of it. Why *do* some kids want to make other peoples' lives miserable? One little thing, just one little thing, and they are on at you ever afterwards, laughing with the others about you, pointing and whispering; being cruel.

I was happier in Hugh Miller's world. But the clocks still ticked and I still woke sometimes to hear them chime the hour and there would be a cold feeling like I'd swallowed the stethoscope. What was going to happen when I was well again? What was going to *happen* … to me?

One morning, when I was half asleep, watching the dust dancing in a shaft of sunlight I heard my grandfather's voice. He sounded angry. There was nobody else's voice, just long spaces that told me he was on the telephone. I felt I could get up. I felt I *should* get up. My legs were like bits of string, but I managed to get my dressing gown on and get myself down the steep attic stairs to the kitchen.

'I will not allow it!' my grandfather was saying loudly. 'I will *forbid* it!' But then he saw me, and his face changed from angry to something else. 'And this conversation is at an *end*,' he finished. He didn't exactly slam the phone down, but he wasn't gentle with it either.

'And what are *you* doing down here?' he demanded.
'I … I just felt a bit better …' I said. But that was all I managed before a hot cloud seemed to cover the room and I had to reach for a chair to keep me up. My grandfather caught me. His touch was gentle.
'Hey, laddie!' he said, helping me to sit down. 'I think you rushed things a bit there!'

I looked at him. He looked right back at me, but I knew better than to ask any questions. We just looked.

He was the first to turn away. 'Would you be wanting some soup?'

he asked briskly? 'Ye need to get your strength up.' Suddenly the remembered taste of Heinz tomato soup flooded my mouth and I knew that was indeed just what I did want. There was fresh bread too — he must have been out to the bakery — and eggs that he told me he had got from the van as it came past from the farm. 'Fresh, they are,' he noted with some satisfaction. 'Straight out of the hen.' That should have put me off the eggs, but I was too hungry by then. I ate everything. My grandfather watched me with what, for him, was approval.

But when I was finished, and the pan was in soak and the bread carefully put back in the big old brown crock he kept for that purpose, he looked a bit alarmed, as if he didn't know what to do next. Into the silence, the phone rang again. He let it ring. Ten times it rang — I counted — and he sat as if turned to stone. I didn't say anything. I had a feeling I knew who was at the other end of the line.

When it stopped, my grandfather reached out blindly for the book on the table. 'Would you like a wee bit more of the story?' he asked. I nodded.

Back in young Hugh's world it was the kind of day when spring really gets a hold over winter and shakes it about a bit. I looked out of the window; like today. Hugh was busy with his education, his way. It was the kind of education I could get to like too. The title of his book still wasn't snappy, but I understood now that he was talking about life and how that teaches you — even when you aren't expecting, or wanting it to.

I closed my eyes while my grandfather read and this time his words were a river that I once watched on a Saturday afternoon, long ago, when there was nothing in the world to bother me and the smell of cut grass was in the air and the taste of ginger beer. Cool.

Hugh didn't mess about. He might not pay much attention to school, but he worked hard at his other stuff. He was still interested in rocks and stones and pebbles. 'I soon,' he said, 'acquired an enviable quickness in distinguishing the different kinds of rock.'

But he didn't know what they were called or how they were made — or how they got to be lying where they were. He began to wonder though, and think about it, and store up in his mind bits of knowledge that would come in handy later.

He got a hammer too, one that his mother told him was more than a hundred years old — his grandfather's hammer — so he could crack at the rocks and see what he could find out. My grandfather's voice was almost laughing while he read how young Hugh found some sheets of beautiful black mica and made sunglasses for himself by putting them between some ordinary mica. That was amazing! And he found some stones that he thought were the same as the red ones in his mother's little brooch, but his neighbours told him they were worthless. 'Those are just stones upon the shore!' they said. I wondered if they had been rubies or even just garnets. Maybe I would find some too.

I knew without a doubt that I was going to walk those paths that Hugh had walked, and climb those cliffs. I was! I would! I wanted to taste the wild raspberries and lie on the fresh green bracken and most of all I wanted the feel of a stone and a hammer and the *crack* of the one on the other. If I imagined it, I could feel what it would be like, the hardness of it and the suddenness of it, and the knowing if you had done it right and the stone would split just the way you wanted it too, and the warm feeling when you got it right. I *knew*!

It took some time. I was impatient to start, but my grandfather made me take it slowly. The ghost-girl helped. Alice. She kept on coming round, even though I wasn't really sick any more. She just appeared every afternoon after school and pretty much stayed there until suppertime. I wondered if she was lonely? She said so little that it was hard to work out, but she seemed to enjoy reading, right enough — and she seemed to enjoy Hugh Miller too.

'Aren't you worried you'll catch my virus?' I asked her once.

'Had it,' she answered. She spoke about as much as my grandfather. Maybe it's a Scottish thing?

My grandfather didn't seem to mind her. He even seemed to like having her there — or maybe it made it easier for him not to talk about some of the things we didn't talk about. Sometimes those things tried to break out of the iron safe inside my mind where I had locked them away. I ignored them.

'Phone's broken,' he said one day when he caught me looking at it. An almost-smile flickered across his face. 'Maybe I put it down too hard.' So it didn't ring, and I stopped listening to the ticking and the gonging of time and lost myself.

CHAPTER FIVE

Sometimes I found myself staring at the telephone. When would it ring? What was she doing, my mother? What would happen? And *why* didn't she ring? That was the only question with an answer. When I looked at it more closely, the wire had been disconnected. I left it as it was. I was disconnected too … and I liked it that way.

No telephones in Hugh Miller's young day. His mother must have wondered where he was sometimes, when he was gone until after dark, up on the hills or — surely worse for her — exploring on the seashore and on the cliffs. More and more I longed to be out there too. Each day was more glorious as the spring moved towards summer. At first, I was only able to take short walks down to the seashore, my knees trembling with effort. I had to stop quite often, mostly to look at bees more closely, — I told myself — or examine the shades of seaweed on the rocks, or do other Hugh Millerish things.

I watched the inflatable boat charging around the Cromarty Firth taking tourists out to look for dolphins. There were dinghies waiting for wind at weekends, fisherman with rods carried hopefully over their shoulders. Old ladies with dogs got to nodding at me and saying what a nice day it had turned out. Sometimes I had to sit down on a bench for a bit, just to rest.

I was surprised by how weak I was. But at last my grandfather allowed me a bit more freedom.

It was only on condition that the ghost-girl came too. I didn't really care. It wasn't *horrible* having her around. Maybe this was what it felt like to have a younger sister? One who didn't nag or make a fuss. My grandfather watched us go. I could feel him looking at my back. 'Mind yourselves on the cliffs!' he shouted out after us. I waved to show that we would. How did he know where I wanted to go?

There were caves in the cliffs. I knew that from several adventures young Hugh had up there, and I really wanted to see them for myself. I'd never been in a cave although children in nearly every book I'd read when I was young seemed to find them all the time. The Famous Five and all that lot practically *lived* in caves.

Hugh's caves are along the line of two great hills called The Sutors that guard the entrance to the Cromarty Firth and protect Cromarty harbour. Some of them are higher up, and Hugh Miller says this is because the sea level was higher long ago. Why? I made a mental note to find out. Hugh probably had. The others were nearer the sea that was still busy carving them out with its waves. There were stalactites in some of them. Stalactites! I thought I would start with one of the easier ones

… but there was a really difficult one that I had set my heart on seeing when I was stronger.

I stopped, suddenly winded. The ghost-girl stopped too.
'Tired?' she asked.
'No,' I said (I have Scottish blood too).

I was looking at the line of the old sea coast — I could clearly see where a cliff behind Cromarty marked where the sea used to be — Hugh Miller talks about it in his book. I was thinking. When Hugh was my age, nobody knew anything much about the theories we learn even in primary school today. In Hugh's time, people were thinking and looking and wondering about what they were finding — all over the place. My grandfather told me about discoveries of seashells high in mountains that were far from the sea and strange marks gouged out of solid rock. How did those shells get there? What made the scrape marks in the rocks? It was a time of questions, right enough — and none with any obvious answers. What was going on? Would thinking about the way the world worked have to be changed?

The ghost-girl was still looking at me. Her eyes were silver again today. She had a very pale, fine kind of face. She didn't smile a lot. I told her what I was thinking about. It seemed only fair when she was the only reason my grandfather was letting me out. She was wearing a T-shirt and skirt that matched the colours of the sea behind her so that she kind of fitted in to the landscape.

'Hmm,' she said. I thought she was going to stop there, but she didn't. 'I *wish* I'd been alive then,' she said. 'I *wish* I had been able to look at the land and have ideas about it — like Hugh Miller did.'

It was the longest speech she had made so far. Two little frown lines appeared between her silver eyes with the effort of it. We walked on.

We both began to speak at the same time. 'How ...'
We laughed. I think she had surprised herself. She certainly surprised me. I showed her that she should go first.

'How did they ever work out what was going on under the earth?' she said after a moment. 'How could they look up there,' and she waved her arm in the direction of The Sutors, 'and work out what was underneath?'
'That's what I was going to say!'
She looked at me sideways and there was just the smallest beginning of a smile.

Find *out*, I told myself. Be like Hugh. Make it your business to know.

To be truthful, I *was* tired. My legs still wobbled. But luckily there were plenty of things to look at and Alice was patient. When I stopped, she stopped. When I looked at a stone, she looked at it too. It was kind of nice.

It was like seeing the film of a book I'd read. We walked along and we walked along and everything was just so ... well, it might sound soppy to say, but it was so beautiful. The long rain and the snow and ice of winter had washed and polished every surface so that it shone.

We went down past the harbour and onto a little beach that stretches round towards the Sutors. I was measuring them against my wobbling legs. Not yet ... but soon. I had a sudden flashback to my grandfather's voice telling me that the Sutors might have been named after two shoemaker brothers (sutor being a Scottish word for shoemaker) throwing tools across the water to each other. My mind suddenly seemed to be filled with things I didn't really need to know.

Stones were lying all over the beach, some of them half-covered with seaweed, Hugh Millerish stones. This was where he had found fossils. I picked some stones up, and so did Alice. We tried banging some together. They were pretty hard. Before, it would never in a million years have occurred to me to bring a hammer along with me and crack one open, like Hugh did when he was young. I wondered if it was difficult? I wondered if it was allowed? I wondered if my grandfather would let me borrow his hammer? He would be sure to have one. The price would probably be a short (or long) speech about: 'neither a borrower nor a lender be,' but it would be worth it.

'My Uncle Ian,' Alice said suddenly, 'is a geology student. At Aberdeen University.'
I stopped banging stones together and turned to look at her. 'What?'
'A geology student,' she repeated carefully. 'Studying rocks,' she added in case I was dafter than she thought. 'Earth Science.'
'Oh,' I said stupidly.
'Maybe … maybe we can ask him how to crack the rocks, like Hugh Miller did.'

I nearly hugged her. Luckily I stopped myself, just in time. 'That would be great,' I said, casual as I could manage. 'Will you ask him?'
She smiled. 'I will.'

And then the shadows got cooler and the sun went behind a cloud and suddenly I wanted to be back on my bed again, maybe with my eyes shut and maybe even with somebody reading me bits of *Schools and Schoolmasters*.

'I'm tired,' said Alice. I think I should go back now. So we did, with only a small look back at the place where the caves would be.

The postie — I mean the postman, I must be careful not to start speaking Scottish — was at the window of my grandfather's kitchen when we got back. They don't use the perfectly good post-box with 'Letters' written on it in faded blue paint. No, they have a system, my grandfather and the postie. Letters coming in are left on the kitchen counter and if my grandfather has a bill to pay, he leaves the stamped addressed envelope clipped onto an old bulldog clip on the window frame and the postie posts it for him. Neat, hey?

Something, I think it was the electricity bill my grandfather had been complaining about, was on its way out. Something else was on its way in, something in a blue envelope that I recognised. It, and a few more like it, had been in our desk drawer for weeks now, waiting for something to need posting. It would be from my mother.

After Alice had gone, I looked at the envelope for a long time. My grandfather was out. Maybe he had gone to get groceries? He didn't go out much otherwise, but sometimes he took his car and drove to a village where they had a supermarket, with more Heinz tomato soup and stuff than they had in the shop here in Cromarty.

The blue envelope stared at me, dared me to. It was my Mum's handwriting all right. It wasn't addressed to me. Even just on the envelope it looked angry. The Famous Five would have had the kettle on and be steaming the envelope open in a minute. I thought about it. Then I didn't. I just sat and looked at it while the kitchen slowly turned darker and my heart with it. The golden afternoon now seemed far away.

I thought about school. I thought about Mr Maggs and the others, the ones who bullied me. There was Malcolm Todd —- always had been, right since we started primary school together. He was the ringleader, the worst of the bullies. But even with him always around, school was bearable until Maggs came — before, but not afterwards. It's not as if I'm worst in the class, well, not at everything anyway. I'm good at English and not bad at History and Geography. I manage to keep up in most things — except maths and of course we have to get *him* for Maths. And he is our class teacher, which is probably the worst because he has to see me every morning, first thing, and I have to see him.

'Ah,' he sneers, 'Little Alexander, the son of the famous Mr Alexander, who has done so much for our community!' He never calls me Jamie, or even James like some of the teachers, just my surname, my dad's name. On and on and on he goes, little things … needling things, things that hurt. 'Off in a dream are we, Alexander? I wonder *what* you dream about? Thinking about your famous Dad, maybe?' And the class would laugh, because they knew what he was on about, siding with him. I would just sit there, taking it, but boiling inside. And the worst was that he knew — he knew what I really *was* thinking about. So did the others. That's what made it so bad.

I remembered Hugh Miller and the day he finally snapped and left school after the beating from his schoolmaster. Mr Maggs never hit me — never laid a finger on me — but it was the same, really as being beaten. He just beat my mind instead of my body. Maybe I could learn from life like Hugh did? Maybe I could read and read and read until I knew everything I needed to know and not *have* to go back to school? Hugh managed. He learned enough on his own to become an important man of his time — famous even. I could get somebody to help me with Maths (I'd never manage that on my own). Of course Hugh Miller had his uncles … but I had my grandfather. Maybe he was good with numbers? That made me think for a moment.

Hugh Miller's uncles had done all kinds of things, read all kinds of things; seen all kinds of things. Uncle Sandy had been in the Royal Navy and had travelled … everywhere, Egypt even — Geography. Uncle James knew about local legends and traditions — History. Where might my grandfather have been? Maybe he would know enough … and I could stay here? Maybe I could ask him?

But then I thought about 'the system' that was already out to get me because of what I had done, and I realised that would never work. Not now, not today when children were loaded around with health and safety regulations and truancy records and a paper trail of everything they did wrong from the age of one. There was no escape from it. Somebody would eventually come round in a van, with a clipboard and a laptop with all of me inside it. Then I'd never get away again.

The door crashed open and there was my grandfather with a couple of supermarket bags. 'I stopped at the bakery and got some of those oatcakes you like …' he started to say, and then he looked where I was looking and saw the envelope. He seemed … well, guilty.

'We'll have a cup of tea,' he said. So we did. The envelope stared at us while we drank it. My grandfather sighed. 'I'd better open it,' he said.

CHAPTER SIX

My mother had not calmed down since I had been sent up here. I could see that from the way her writing dug into the page, spitting the dots on every 'i' and slashing every 't'. My grandfather read in silence. Then he sighed. 'She's coming,' he said heavily. 'She's not pleased.'

He looked at me. Just like with Alice this afternoon — there was a quiver of a smile at the corner of his mouth. 'Week after next,' he said. 'Friday. When your mother gets back from a business trip to Amsterdam.' He heaved himself out of his chair by its arms and went over to the telephone. 'May as well plug this thing in again,' he said, 'no stopping her now. She phoned Mrs McBain,' he added, watching the kettle, 'her with the old Labrador. So she knows we're alive. She says she expects I've unplugged the phone.' He looked out of the window. 'I've done it before.'

My mother is quite a gentle woman, but when she gets mad … well, you don't want to know about it. My grandfather looked as if he already did. 'Just like *her* mother,' he said gloomily. 'Just like her.'

He unpacked the groceries, taking his time so I would notice. There were six different kinds of Heinz soup, including tomato. There were some frozen pies, different kinds. There were chocolate biscuits. He looked to see if I was watching. 'Only for special occasions,' he said, 'not for everyday.' Then he hesitated before he broke open the packet. 'And for days when we need cheering up.' We both chewed on our biscuits for a while. 'Or strengthening.'

He took his time getting settled with *Schools and Schoolmasters* after supper. I washed the soup plates and put the pot in soak. He put the coal on the fire himself — just to be sure. I sat down and waited while he searched around for something in the book. Then we had the usual throat clearing for a while and then he got stuck in.

What he read to me was incredible. It was Hugh Miller imagining another world — a world of millions of years ago; a world nobody could ever have seen because there were no people then to see it. I was, as Hugh Miller said himself somewhere else in his book, 'lost in astonishment and admiration.' It was the world of the coal forests — forests that made the black stuff we were currently burning in the grate, black stuff that was maybe three hundred and fifty *million* years old, my grandfather said. It was a quietening thought:

In this swampy landscape there were '... long withdrawing lakes fringed with dense thickets of the green Calamite, tall and straight as the masts of pinnaces, and inhabited by enormous fishes, that glittered through the transparent depths in their enamelled armour of proof; or glades of thickest verdure, where the tree fern mingled its branch-like fronds with the hirsute arms of gigantic club moss, and where, amid strange forms of shrub and tree no longer known on earth, the stately Araucarian reared its proud head two hundred feet over the soil …'

My grandfather looked at me over the top of his glasses. 'You know of course that Calamites are giant leafy horsetails? he asked. 'And Araucarians were great spiky trees like monkey-puzzles? A few weeks ago, I would just have shrugged. Now I asked to see the words.

They were difficult to read. The sentences were very long and the words were long too — I had never heard of some of them. But it rolled over me like waves of beautiful sound when my grandfather read it to me. Hugh Miller went on to write about fish that were thirty to forty feet in length, with teeth three times as big as even the biggest alligator. It made you think. Where did they go? What happened to the forests that once were here in Scotland? I thought, with a little shiver, that I would rather be here *now*.

When he had finished, my Grandfather put down the book and closed it gently. 'It is time,' he said slowly, ' to look at things a little differently. Time to change.' He examined me over the top of his glasses. 'Hugh Miller did.' He kept on looking at me. I didn't look away, as I would have done only three weeks ago. I looked right back. 'Yes,' I said, 'differently.'

There was a little silence, broken only by the hissing and spitting of the ancient coal on the fire. My grandfather gave it a shake with the poker. 'The way I look at it, we have just over a week to make a change.' I nodded. 'By the time your mother — my daughter — gets here, there has to be something for her to see that will please her. Otherwise,' and he looked straight at me again, 'you will be leaving here. She is talking about ... well, talking about sending you somewhere you won't be able to get into such messes. To a school for youngsters with ... problems.' He looked away for a moment. 'I don't think either of us want that.'

My heart sank. This had been spoken of before ... when the trouble all started. 'I can't manage,' she had said, her face white as the wall behind her. 'It's too much for me ... on my own.' In the room with us was a silent, angry presence, my father. Neither of us spoke about him, but I knew, from the shape of her mouth, that he was there, in her mind as he often was. I didn't have any words. She sighed, but she didn't cry, not that time. I didn't want either of us to have to go back to that.

She pulled me gently towards her, so I was staring into her wide-open eyes. She looked more worried than I had ever seen her — frightened almost. '*Tell me,*' she said, her eyes fixed on mine. 'Tell me!' But I couldn't. When I tried to say anything — anything at all — about Georgie Crawford and what happened to him, about the school bullies and how they made my life hell … about Mr Maggs and his endless tormenting … the words turned to lumps of mud in my mouth. I just shook my head. There *were* no words.

My grandfather was eyeing the letter on the table.
'What can we do?' I asked him.
'I have a plan,' he told me. I nodded hopefully. 'We will do a project — that's what they call them, isn't it? On Hugh Miller.'

It was not quite what I had been thinking, but it had its good side. He was looking at me again. 'Sleeping on it. That's the thing. Tomorrow we will make our decision. Over breakfast.'
'Yes.'
'Now …' he glanced at the clock (the fast one), 'it's bedtime for you. Goodnight.'

I went to sleep immediately I had got the bed warm enough. No thinking around, stirring at the pot of ideas and worries. Nothing. No nightmares. Sleep.

When I woke up, I cautiously investigated the day and my own mind. It looked surprisingly good. The day was raining — but it was Scotland after all. My mind was … well; it seemed ready for new things and new ideas. It seemed optimistic for the first time in a while. Maybe it was the chocolate biscuit. I got up, got dressed and went downstairs.

My grandfather was stirring the porridge. Thoughtfully. 'Hurry up,' he said, plonking the bowl down on the kitchen table. 'We have things to do.'

What we had to do first was go to the museum — the Hugh Miller museum. It is only about three minute's walk from the cottage, up a little lane and into the main street. We could see the Hugh Miller statue towering over Cromarty. It reminded me that Hugh Miller was not just a boy like me, but a man who had a big voice in the Scotland of his day. My grandfather stopped for a breather when we got to the top of the lane, eyes fixed on Mr Miller on his column.

'Jamie …' his voice trailed away in a question, unlike his usual decisive way of speaking. 'Jamie … it is not good to listen to another man's dreams. I learned that in the army. But I'm afraid I have listened to yours. When you were sick. When you were in a fever and talking … saying things you have not said to me.' I looked down at the ground. 'But if you have listened … to another man's dreams … then you have to confess. Otherwise it is dishonest.'

I stopped looking at the ground and turned to look at my grandfather. He took my breath away. He didn't have to tell me that! He could have just kept quiet. Then I began to worry. What had I said?

'Nothing I had not already imagined,' he answered my unspoken question. 'I am sorry I was not around.' His face hardened. 'I am sorry your *father* was not around.' We both looked at the ground this time. 'But I am here now.'

He clapped me on the shoulder, so hard that I nearly lost my balance. I think he was confusing me with one of his army buddies; the ones who talked in their dreams. 'Right. Let's get at it.'

The Hugh Miller Museum is yellow and golden and quite modern. In it are things that I had not expected to see, and things I could never have known about. It was a careful sort of a place. The people who had made this had cared about Hugh Miller.

The lady in charge that day was very kind. She knew my grandfather and now she knew me. 'You won't take everything in on the first day,' she said. 'It might look small, but there is a lot in here.' She smiled at my grandfather. 'Mr Ross can tell you that. He has been here so many times, and he still comes back!'

They went and had a cup of tea. I could hear them out in the garden that was new, named after Hugh Miller's wife, Lydia. Wife? I was still in the days of his schoolroom and the games on the hillside. They were talking about the volunteers working on the garden on Saturdays. Neither of them mentioned my name.

I wandered about, looking at this and looking at that. But I was focused now. My grandfather was right. We needed to show my mother something when she came. We needed to show her a sense of purpose and change. I had to sharpen up.

I looked at the pictures of Hugh Miller. Nobody wears whiskers like that any more! And his hair seemed to spring up as if it was excited about something. His head was really large — maybe because he had a bigger brain than usual. Everybody seemed to think he was a genius. Yes, it sure was a big head … but his eyes … in all the photographs of him (and these were taken in the very early days of photography and were called calotypes, it said in a little printed note) his eyes seemed to look straight out into the future. Or maybe he was looking back into the past? Maybe he was looking at Deep Time, and wondering. In those days, if you collected fossils and rocks and thought about what you found — at all — you had to be thinking about how the world had happened to end up the way it is, and that way was not likely to be exactly what it says in the Bible. It must have been scary. My grandfather says that thinking people everywhere were beginning to see that what was written there wasn't literal.

'So six days could mean six … ages or something?' I asked.
'Hmm.' He stopped for a moment. 'There's no easy answers to any of those kinds of questions, but yes, I think so. There were those who believed that every single word of the Bible had to be

true — still *are* many who think that. And there were those who could see with their own eyes that much, much more time had to be allowed for if the evidence they were finding in the rocks could be believed.'

I thought about that. 'It must have been difficult for them,' I said at last. My grandfather smiled at me. He has a very kind smile when he remembers to use it. 'Right, laddie! It *was* very hard — and not always popular with the crowd! Hugh Miller wrote an enormous amount about fossils and time and the rocks, but he was a true Christian at the same time. Some people found that hard — Hugh seemed to be able to manage it.'

Not for the first time, I wondered what it was like to be Hugh Miller. What went on inside his head as he walked — and he walked hard and fast over long distances all his life? What did he think about all this? He couldn't have just stored everything away 'for later'. Could he?

In the museum I started to see Hugh Miller in another way altogether. In this building, he was a man, and an important one. Here he was remembered as a newspaper editor and a writer, someone who influenced public opinion by what he wrote, twice a week — articles on every kind of topic but he also wrote about things that stayed with him from his childhood, like the stories of the old times and tales his mother must have told him; tales from the old people about the old times.

Hugh Miller wrote with a steel nib pen that you had to dip into ink all the time. I'd seen one before, in another museum somewhere. They were pretty modern in Hugh's day — before that they used quill pens made out of feathers — and were very messy if you weren't careful. You could easily make blots with the ink and spoil a whole page. You made blots all the time anyway, and people then had boxes of fine sand to sprinkle on the wet ink. I had to think about that. We use computers at school most of the time and Mum has a laptop at home that I can use for checking the Internet and typing stuff. I wondered if my grandfather had a steel-nib pen around the place? Maybe he had written with one when he was at school? I made a note to ask him.

The lady was right. There was way too much to take in on one day. I concentrated on Hugh Miller the writer. There was a little magazine about Cromarty that he had made when he was seventeen. There was only the one copy — ever — but he did every page himself. I stood for a long time, just looking at his handwriting. Hugh Miller did this with his own hand — with ink and a steel-nib pen!

The other thing that made me think were the copies of his big newspaper called *The Witness*, that he did when he was grown up and lived in Edinburgh. It came out twice a week and was one of the better selling Scottish newspapers, in the days when they didn't have television to tell them everything.

The pages were so big that they must have been difficult to turn and printed in such tiny print that it was hard to read. There were no pictures and advertisements to break up the page either, just words and words and words. The lady came in then and explained some things — like how important newspapers were in those days and how respected Hugh Miller was — and how very hard he worked. He wrote about ten thousand words a week when he was really busy! I don't know if I can believe that! Sometimes when Miss Edgar sets us compositions for homework, I watch the word count on Mum's laptop crawling along. Five *hundred* is a lot! I came out of there really impressed. Really, *really* impressed.

My grandfather was waiting for me at the door. He glanced at the sky. 'Tomorrow,' he announced, 'which is Saturday, will begin with light rain. There might be some sun about midday. So we are going to follow a path that Hugh Miller walked, with his mother. It is about thirty-three miles.' He glanced at me. 'And because you are still in recovery, we will go in the car instead of walking.' I gulped. And we will take Alice with us. She could do with an outing.'

I think that, as I followed him back down the lane, my mouth might have been open.

I liked doing projects at school. Of course, when one was scheduled, I groaned with the rest of the class, but I secretly enjoyed the planning, the planning and the research.

'We must make a careful plan,' my grandfather said. 'And then do meticulous research.' I didn't say anything, but maybe I smiled a little because he looked at me quite sharply. 'But I suppose you know about that.'

I realised that if I was going to have any voice in this project, I'd better get involved. I got a notebook out of my rucksack. 'Right,' I said. 'Let's start.' It was a bit like the beginning of a soccer match when you find out who your opposition player is going to be and jostle around a bit to find out how good he is. My grandfather was good.

I drew three columns on the first page and made headings, Geologist, Writer and Person. My grandfather looked over my shoulder. 'And Editor,' he pointed out. 'That's too important to miss out.' I squeezed in another column, a bit narrower. He noticed. 'You'll be needing a bit more space for that,' he remarked.

I asked him about the steel-nib pen then, and if he had used a quill pen too but he just gave me a look. 'I,' he said, a little stiffly, used a dipping pen with a metal nib when I started school. I'm not *that* old.'

CHAPTER SEVEN

Scotland, Hugh Miller's Scotland. My grandfather spoke of it with such love as we drove the winding road to the north. I listened to his voice embroidering the landscape we were looking at with his own memories; I realised that I did not know him at all. He spoke of times before I was born, friends long gone; girls he had known, girls he had maybe kissed. Farms that had been sold and farms that had been kept in families.

Alice sat in the back. She was listening too. I could feel her listening and — almost — feel her smiling. Her bright red anorak, and her smile, seemed to cheer up the day.

'Of course, when Hugh Miller walked up here,' my grandfather said, getting back to the matter in hand, ' it would have been very different. Och, yes, very different!' He sounded much more Scottish than he usually did. 'There would not have been as many trees,' he shook his head. 'Hugh Miller and his mother would have walked through a much wilder countryside and they would have followed tracks and paths well-worn through the heather and the bracken.' He waved an arm at the farmland and woods. 'This is all new, since then,' he said. 'This all came with The Improvements — when the owners of the land began to change it, so that *they* could make more money.' I could feel a short lecture coming on — or a long one. 'It was a time of change, Hugh's time.'

He was silent for a bit, driving carefully; looking at the road. 'I don't think it is written about enough,' he said. 'But people suffered up here, before and during — and after — Hugh Miller's time.' He stopped speaking again and Alice and I were silent too. 'It was happening elsewhere,' he said softly after a time. 'But these were *my* people, my ancestors and they had it very hard, aye, very hard.'

I knew that from the readings. Times were impossibly difficult and life was changing everywhere — everywhere in Europe — and especially for the poor folk. Industry was coming, factories and towns with nowhere decent for people to live, no proper schools, no hospitals or health care, no comfort at all. Hugh Miller had a lot to say about the Clearances, how the Highlanders were cleared off their land and forced to live in another way — or in another place; like Canada, for example. Change, change, change … Change was one thing that hadn't changed. From the time of Hugh Miller's beautiful Carboniferous forests, to last week, change was sure to be happening. Hugh could imagine the forests of deep time, but could he have imagined now?

'Aye. It was hard to live on the land, but it was harder to lose it, my grandfather added. His mood had changed. He had been bright and busy when we left Cromarty. Now sadness weighed on him. 'The big landlords brought in new ideas. Improvements! Well they *improved* the people right off the land, people who had lived there for generations. Many a family found themselves scraping a living from trying-to-fish when the fish were gone, or moved off to farming land that was not enough for any poor person to survive off.' He shook his head. 'And there were the ill years — times when the crops failed; and the cholera came.'

I felt the cold finger of the drowned woman touch me again and I shivered. Maybe my grandfather noticed. He looked at Alice in the mirror and cracked a smile. 'Are you fine in the back, then?' he asked.

'Yes, thank you,' she said politely.

He smiled at her again. 'Good,' he said. 'Good.'

I was glad she was there.

Hugh and his mother went to visit her sister in a place called The Barony of Gruids — a journey Hugh made three times as a boy. It must have been like going abroad. He had gone to a place where everybody spoke Gaelic, instead of the Scots he was used to, and customs and culture were very different, even such a short distance from his home. I thought about our school trip to France. I hadn't understood a word anyone said to me and had been pretty dazed by the way everything was different … within only a few miles of the English coast.

'Hugh was always sorry that he didn't have the Gaelic,' my grandfather said.' (I had been a bit sorry I didn't have the French.

Maybe I should have listened to Miss Morris a bit more.) But Hugh Miller must have known some, I thought, spending summers up here with his wild cousins.

Gruids sounded like a fun kind of a holiday. Once he and his mother got there, young Hugh was out on the moors and up on the mountains with his cousin George, mostly. There is a word picture of the other cousin, William, who made a bit of money in trade in Edinburgh, with some of what my grandfather called 'fancy friends'. They were only fancy as long as the money lasted, but they had a good time while it did.

George was a stonemason - and Hugh Miller must have liked what he saw. Stonemasons couldn't work in the worst of the winter and Hugh saw the gap for a few months of reading and learning when it was too cold to break and cut stones and lay them. It changed Hugh's life when he met George — maybe because he only saw the good bits, when George was resting from the hard labour of the other part of the year. And George sounds like fun — somebody who stirred things up and maybe was a bit of a hero to a boy like Hugh. He was probably taking time off in the summer because there was no work — but Hugh was not taking any notice of that, or of the fact that there was no money for a mason when he wasn't working.

Our purpose today was to find the remains of the cottage where

Hugh's aunt lived — if there were any remains. 'They pulled them down,' my grandfather said sadly. 'Or else they fell down. This place was cleared of folk in the early 1800s — cleared for sheep-farming.' Change. Change. Change. Sitting in the car I had the feeling that Time was elastic, springing back and forwards again. The Clearances seemed like last week and Hugh Miller seemed like now.

Hugh Miller was younger than I am when he made the journey first. I wondered if he had looked after his mother, or if she had looked after him. They would have eaten what little they had brought with them, my grandfather said, and people along the way would have helped them out — poor people, but used to sharing. They would have slept rough, or maybe sheltered in a cottage. People were used to that then too. It took them two days, so they would have stopped somewhere along the way, or slept under the stars.

We had *Schools and Schoolmasters* with us in the car (of course). We drove about for a bit, trying to find the place from a map and the notes my grandfather had made. When all three of us were *almost* sure we had the place where the cottage was, we stopped. It was very quiet. Faint pinging noises came from under the bonnet of the car and then stopped. Alice found the place in the old red book and read aloud. My grandfather and I listened:

'It was a low, long, dingy edifice of turf, four or five rooms in length but only one in height, that, lying along a gentle acclivity, somewhat resembling, at a distance, a huge black snail creeping up the hill. As the lower apartment was occupied by my uncle's half-dozen milk cows, the declination of the floor proved of signal importance from the free drainage it procured; the second apartment, which was of considerable size, formed the sitting room of the family, and had, in the old Highland style, its fire full in the middle of the floor, without back or sides; so that, like a bonfire kindled in the open air, all the inmates could sit around it.'

We could see the place where it might have been, but there were no ruins. It was hard to imagine people living there — and cows. The women would have sat, Hugh told us in his book, on one side of the fire and the men on the other. Beyond that were very small and dark bedrooms and further on a little cupboard with a window in it where Hugh and his mother slept, beyond that was 'the room,' where William, Hugh's merchant cousin, entertained his friends, and where his books were kept.

Only just over two hundred years ago… and people lived like *that*? Time was stretching again. No mobile phones or computers, no under-floor heating; fires in the middle of the room; cows living practically in the house — with drainage facilities. In the evenings, the family would gather round the fire and the uncle would 'take the Book' and the Bible would be read in Gaelic.

None of us said anything. My grandfather turned the car and we went home.

My grandfather told stories on the way back, ghost stories that Hugh had written in all of his books, really, but mostly in one called *Scenes and Legends*. I was glad that *My Schools and Schoolmasters* was long enough to keep us going for the project. I don't like ghost stories — and these were stories that got right under your skin and into your mind. They seemed … real. As if they came from another different time, a time when people were closer to the land and the elements, listening fearfully, a time before the Book had come to Scotland, or maybe a time when they knew both and were afraid.

Hugh had an adventure up here when he hurt his foot, quite badly at the Falls of Shin, waterfalls from Loch Shin that is near where the cottage was. It was on another visit, one that he made without his mother, but with his younger cousin Walter, who did not know the way.

I would have told somebody that I'd hurt myself — and somebody would have arrived with a first aid kit and a couple of forms to fill in, and done something about it. Hugh was braver than that. He just kept on going, setting out to walk home with his cousin Walter without saying anything about the pain. It must have hurt him quite a lot, because he ended up delirious with fever on a bleak stretch of moor and having to be rescued by elderly people living nearby and then taken home on a cart. Hugh's mother sure had a time with him! My mother came to mind. She sure had a time with me, I supposed.

I had the strangest feeling as we drove back down the road we had come. I felt as if we were leaving Hugh Miller, the boy, behind us. When we got back to Cromarty he would be changed, and changing, into the man he was going to be.

Life as a stonemason was maybe not what Hugh had been expecting after his summer with George. Life was hard for everybody at that time and business was not as good as it had been. Cromarty itself was in what I suppose we would call a recession now. Maybe it didn't come upon them during a six o' clock news, like it does with us, but slowly the business was going. Prices dropped after the wars with France came to an end. The army and navy did not need as much in the way of supplies in peacetime. The herring fishing failed. My grandfather says it was always risky business fishing for herring. Sometimes they just didn't arrive in the season when they should. Nobody knew why. But it made people hungry in the fishermen's cottages and elsewhere.

Bigger things were going on, and all of that must have been hard to see from where Hugh Miller stood on the beach at Cromarty. His uncles tried to persuade him, but he had made up his mind to be a mason, and nothing would stop him.

Hugh made a mistake. Just when he was starting out as a mason, the building jobs were drying up. Big projects were not being started and even small building jobs were scarce. Almost immediately Hugh found himself working — rough work too — away from home. The work was hard. The conditions stonemasons worked under were horrible. After only a short time, Hugh Miller was coughing with the stonemason's lung disease from the dust; coughing up blood.

Alice read aloud to us as we wound our way home, choosing passages that gave us the full effect of Hugh's new life.

It was a job Hugh took great pride in. Every block of stone in a building had to be cut by hand, whether it was for fine buildings in the city or ordinary buildings on the land. Hugh did his time on both and was good at his job — but it did his health no good. Masons slept rough or in very poor conditions and were very poorly fed — mostly on oatmeal in some form or another:

'These barracks or bothies are almost always of a miserable description. I have lived in hovels that were invariably flooded in wet weather by the overflowing of neighbourhood swamps and through whose roofs I could tell the hour at night by marking from my bed the stars that were passing over the openings along the ridge.

I remember that Uncle James, in urging me not to become a mason, told me that a neighbouring laird, when asked why he left a crazy old building standing behind a group of neat modern offices, informed the querist that he found it of great convenience every time his speculations brought a drove of pigs or a squad of masons the way.'

Hugh must have truly treasured his wintertime back in Cromarty with a good roof over his head and better food — and dreaded going back to the rough life of a mason — but he didn't give up. He was a stonemason for five years before his health forced him to turn to the slightly easier work of monumental mason, where he could make sundials and gravestones nearer home.

'What happened then?' I asked. My grandfather and Alice spoke together.
'He fell in love!'
'*Yuch*,' I thought.

CHAPTER EIGHT

In the evenings, we worked on our project, my grandfather and I. We'd stoke the fire up with Carboniferous forest and then my grandfather would read aloud and I would work on my notebook. Sometimes we'd stop and ask each other things. I was learning a lot. Maybe my grandfather was too.

'What is this Facebook nonsense?' he asked once, out of the blue.

'Um, it's a way of keeping in touch with … everybody.'

He looked dubious. 'What? All the time?'

'Yes,' I answered gloomily. 'Yeah. All the time.' I couldn't think of anybody I wanted to be in touch with right now, not one.

Neither could my grandfather. 'Waste of time.' He muttered. 'Waste of time.' He too was happier in Hugh Miller's world.

The columns on our chart were filling up, mostly the one called 'Person'. It took a lot of words to understand Hugh Miller. First he was one thing — then he was another. Who was he really? Maybe I wondered that out loud because my grandfather interrupted my thought.

'He was writing about himself, of course,' he said, 'which is always difficult to do. Looking back at a time when he was a boy from a time when he was a man.' He gave a little laugh. 'I think he smoothed over some of the … rougher bits! I get the feeling he was quite a trial to his uncles and his mother … and more of one to his schoolmasters! Have I told you about the cave?'

I settled back in my chair. The fire was warmer than fires had been when I first came. Stories flowed around the room in its glow — as I suppose stories always have.

'There's a cave,' my grandfather began, 'on the South Sutor.' He grinned. 'We all knew about it — people always did. 'And there was *always* trouble with boys thinking they could get into it, when they couldn't.'
I wondered if my grandfather had been one of those boys?

'You can walk there on certain tides, but they don't happen very often — and you have to be quick having a look round and then get back home before the sea gets you.' He smiled again and I knew suddenly that he *had* been one of those boys.

'Hugh Miller went there with his uncles, sensible men who knew about the tides and would have warned him, aye, most definitely would have warned him. But Hugh knew better of course, and a few days later he took along one of his friends — a younger boy — and they just went to have a look — just a look — from the top. They could see that there was a drop of about twelve feet, but that was nothing to them. They just jumped off — and only when they were standing at the entrance to the cave, did it occur to them to think that they would not be able to jump back up again.'

I thought about it. I had done things like that — not with caves, but with life.

'So they decided they would just have a look around, so long as they were there. In young Hugh's words it was "hard to be disappointed and the caves so near." And it is indeed a wonderful cave. There was plenty to explore and they put right out of their minds the idea that they might have a very long time to enjoy it before they could get home again.'

I looked round the cottage, noticing it again as if for the first time. I looked at my grandfather, lost in the pleasure of the story. I felt strange. Something had … changed. Suddenly I realised what. I was happy.

My grandfather got the book out to refresh his memory — and Hugh Miller wrote it all much better anyway:

'… neither of us understood the philosophy of neap tides at the period. I was quite sure I had got round at low tide with my uncles not a great many days before, and we both inferred that, if we but succeeded in getting round now, it would be quite a pleasure to wait among the caves until such time as the fall of the tides should lay bare a passage for our return.'

It wasn't. Well, it was a pleasure at first:

'The larger cave proved a mine of marvels and we found a great deal additional to wonder at on the slopes beneath the precipices and along the piece of rocky sea-beach in front ... the mysterious and gloomy depths in which plants hardened into stone and water became marble. In a short time, we had broken off with our hammers whole pocketfuls of stalactites and petrified moss...even the pigeons, as they shot whizzing by, one moment scarce visible in the gloom, next radiant in the light — all acquired a new interest from the peculiarity of the *setting* in which we saw them.'

It did seem a *little* ominous when the tide began to creep up the beach, but the two boys just carried on hoping that the change of the tide would fix all that, and went on exploring.

The sun began to set. Everything turned a nasty grey colour, preparing for night. Every creature that had wings made use of them to speed off home — but the boys could not; they were trapped by the tide.

They tried to climb up to the place they had so easily jumped from, but it had never been done before and was not going to happen now. They were stuck.

'Wouldn't care for myself,' said the younger boy, bursting into tears, 'if it were not for my mother, but what will my mother say?'

I thought about the feeling Hugh must have had — that sinking feeling when you know you have done something really, *really* stupid, and there is no way back:

> 'The rising wind began to howl mournfully amid the cliffs, and the sea, hitherto silent, to beat heavily against the shore, and to boom, like distress guns, from the recesses of the two deep-sea caves. We could hear too the beating rain, now heavier, now lighter, as the gusts swelled or sank ...'

It would have been bad enough, as the two boys made what beds they could out of dried grass, but when the smaller boy fell asleep, Hugh was tormented by the memory of a drowned sailor who had washed up on the beach about a month before. All the boys had gone to have a look. Now Hugh was haunted by what he had seen. Every time he dropped off to sleep, he was quickly woken by dreams of that horrible sight and could not sleep. I tried to push the scene he had so vividly described out of my mind too, but it would not go away. I imagined him sleepless on the ledge, the sound of the waves pounding on the beach below; the memory of his drowned father.

Luckily, around midnight, the noise of the storm dropped and they crept to the edge to see how the tide looked down on the beach. It was no better. Suddenly Hugh realised the seriousness of their situation. It would be a *week* before they could get out, not a twelve-hour tide!

They shouted out in fear and in despair when they spotted the lights of a boat — one that they later learned was loaded with stone and had no smaller boat with which to rescue them, and they thought they heard a faint yell in answer, but could not be certain.

Eventually, when the ghost of the dead sailor finally allowed Hugh some rest and he slept at last, the boys were woken by voices shouting down to them and discovered half the village out to rescue them and fearing them dead.

We sat quiet for a bit after that, my grandfather and I, imagining.

Of course Hugh Miller, who was always one to bounce back, wrote a poem about the experience, which was passed around the place and attracted a lot of attention as a result. I would have thought he had enjoyed enough of that when he was lost in a sea cave and feared dead.

I told Alice about it the next day, a glorious Saturday of freedom from school for her. We were on our way to look for The Moss of the Willows and see if there were any more elk horns to be collected. She was quiet for a moment.

'So what did *you* do?' Alice asked.

We were sitting on the bank of a stream, with our feet in the slippery, silvery water by then. 'What?' I said.

She was patient. 'Hugh Miller got into trouble in a cave. What did *you* do? Why were you sent up here when it isn't even school holidays?'

My mind went into Deep Time. It had been doing that more and more, recently. It hesitated around the coal swamps for a bit and then it zoomed back to almost-now, watching Malcolm Todd tormenting me in the space between school and home, the space where no teachers ever seemed to go, the space where I never wanted to be again. It hovered around Georgie Crawford for a bit, on the day they dared — bullied — him to walk along the roof-ridge of the sports store, and then it lifted off and zoomed somewhere else, somewhere where Malcolm Todd would never matter again, unless I let him.

'I set fire to the school,' I told Alice.

There was a still moment, one when nothing happened. Then she laughed, and everything hung on that moment; and changed. Change.

What!' she said, and it wasn't a question. There was some admiration in her voice.

'I set fire to the school,' I said again, calmly. Suddenly it didn't seem like such an important thing to have done, such a Big Thing. 'In the science lab, with a Bunsen burner; one night.'

This time she laughed quite loudly, like she really meant it. Then she was quiet. 'Why?' she asked. Nobody had asked me that. Not once. It had all been hushed up — too much paperwork I had thought. It hadn't been much of a fire, after all; too *much* bother. I took a deep breath.

'Because I had had enough.'
She considered that. When she spoke again, her voice was soft, like a whisper. 'What did they do to you?'

My mind was still. I thought about it. 'They hurt me,' I said at last. She didn't need to know how.

In the quiet of the stream and the water and the slippery silvery feel of it on our feet, she touched my arm with one of her thin fingers. 'I'm sorry,' she said.

It was ... it was fine.

Alice told me that, if we went to the beach at Eathie next weekend, where Hugh collected some of his first fossils, we would see her Uncle Ian, the geology student, working on the beach. I couldn't think of anything I would rather do.

'Can my grandfather come too?' I asked after a moment. 'Already asked him,' she said. Which was lucky because it meant we could go in his car.

He laughed when he noticed his own hammer sticking out of the waistband of my jeans. 'Hoping for an undiscovered species?' he asked. I just smiled, but I was; secretly I was.

Reading about fossils is a lot different from actually being in a place where they might be. I could feel a kind of tingling in my spine, an excitement. It was coming up through the ground, through my trainers and socks, up the nerves of my legs and straight in to my heart. There were fossils here. We knew that. People had been coming here and collecting them since Hugh Miller wrote about them in *Scenes and Legends*. The 'in' thing to do in Hugh's day was collecting stuff — wildflowers, tropical fish, shells; stones. People had big cabinets built for their fern collections and tanks for their aquarium fish. There were cupboards in the corner of the drawing room for the 'curiosities' that they either collected themselves, or bought from other collectors. It was a complete craze!

Hugh was interested in stones when he was a boy — all boys are (I am) but Hugh got *really* interested by what he saw, when he was a grown man in a quarry where they were cutting stone. He noticed a sheet of rock that was as hard as ... well, stone, but covered with water ripple marks as if the sea had just rested on it, not a moment before. How had this happened?

' ... what had become of the waves that had thus fretted the solid rock, or of what element had they been composed? I felt as completely at fault as Robinson Crusoe did on his first discovering the print of the man's foot on the sand.'

It was a moment waiting to happen. Just after that, Hugh was working a few miles from Cromarty at a place called Navity. In his lunch break one day, on the beach nearby, he casually broke open one of the bits of limestone littering the beach —

he had the tools and the skills, after all — and found a fossil ammonite:

'Wonderful to relate, it contained inside a beautiful finished piece of sculpture … Was there another such a curiosity in the whole world? I broke open a few other nodules of similar appearance — for they lay pretty thickly on the shore — and found that there might. In one of these were what seemed to be the scales of fishes … in the centre of another was actually a piece of decayed wood. Of all Nature's riddles, these seemed to me to be at once the most interesting and the most difficult to expound.'

I thought about that. I thought about that moment, the moment when Hugh Miller broke open a stone — and found a fossil inside. Was there *indeed* such a curiosity in the world before?

CHAPTER NINE

Of course you can't go around chopping up stones on the beach and taking fossils home with you. (Why had I suspected that all along?) Alice's Uncle Ian laughed at the idea. 'No,' he said kindly, 'this beach at Eathie is protected, otherwise people would come and cart them away by the truck-load and sell them.' He looked across the beach seriously. 'Things have changed since Hugh Miller's time, although fossil collectors have always paid well for good specimens. Anyway,' he added.' You would need to be quite strong and skilful and have the right equipment.' He noticed my hammer. 'And protective eye glasses.'

I sighed (quietly). Change again. But he had a point. And things *had* changed since Hugh Miller's time. There were a lot more people, for one thing, and values had changed. Money values, like how much you could get for a fossil on e-Bay, but important values too, like how important it was to preserve what we know about our planet. Nobody had really begun to think about that in Hugh's day. There was still so *much* of everything then — and fewer people tramping around.

But there were things that we *were* allowed to do, and Ian showed us how. Even my grandfather got excited. Hugh Miller did too, when he first found fossils at Eathie:

'The layers into which the beds readily separate are hardly the eighth part of an inch in thickness, and yet on every layer there are the impressions of thousands and tens of thousands of the various fossils …We may turn over these wonderful leaves one after one, like the leaves of a herbarium and find the pictorial records of a former creation in every page: scallops and gryphites and ammonites, of almost every variety peculiar to the formation, and at least some eight or ten varieties of belemnite; twigs of wood, leaves of plants, cones of an extinct species of pine, bits of charcoal, and the scales of fishes; and as if to render their pictorial appearance more striking, though the leaves of this interesting volume are of a deep black, most of the impressions are of a chalky whiteness. I was lost in admiration and wonder.'

So was I. Ian showed us how to split the layers of shale with fairly simple tools that looked suspiciously like wallpaper scrapers to me. But it was still exciting. We found tiny ammonites and other shells and Ian identified them for us. But I still hankered after a nodule and he knew it.

'I've got a couple of stones over there,' he nodded towards a rock where his bright orange rucksack was perched away from the incoming tide. 'Like to have a look?'

We rock-hopped across to the place. He looked at us for a moment silently, enjoying the moment. Then he adjusted a pair of goggles from round his neck, pulled his own proper geological hammer from his back pocket and efficiently cracked open a piece of limestone.

We were lucky — and Ian was an expert fieldworker — the first nodule contained an ammonite. The wonder of it struck us speechless. We just looked, Alice, my grandfather and I, without saying anything and Ian understood the moment and didn't say anything either. It looked … it looked as though somehow it had just been put inside the stone, glossy and fresh and … *new* looking. I looked up at Ian and he smiled.

'What you have just seen must be the most special moment, ever, for anybody who is interested in geology and fossils,' he said quietly. 'It was for me.'

'It would have been for Hugh Miller,' I said.
Ian nodded. 'Yes. It would have been.'
'How …' I began and Ian laughed softly. 'Everybody asks that question. How did the remains of animals and plants get inside very old rocks?'

I nodded. He looked away for a moment, trying to find words, I thought, that would be easy for us to understand. 'They didn't "get inside." The nodule — that's the proper name for a rock like this — formed around them, inside the mother rock, partly as a result of the chemical changes that happened when the organism decayed.' He looked from one of us to the other. 'That enough for you?'

It wasn't really, but I could see that this was a process so complicated that I might have to go to university before I could understand it.

'Yes,' said my grandfather, who had obviously thought about this before.

'Yes,' said Alice, rather firmly.

Ian laughed again. 'Who can imagine what went through Hugh Miller's mind. He knew some theories about how the world could have been formed — and of course he knew his Bible very well. But he was not, at that time, connected to anyone else in the world that could help him with this. He just examined what he found and stored up the information for later.'

For a moment Ian looked thoughtful — admiring even. 'Over the years Hugh Miller worked something out that turned out to be very important. Over there,' he waved northwards towards The Sutors. 'Hugh worked out that there should be similar fossil beds — and there were fossil beds. That's where he discovered the fossil fishes later that made him famous among those who were interested in such things.' I remembered Alice and I wondering how anyone could work out what was going on under the earth and here Hugh Miller was — doing it. I remembered the top floor of the museum where there were details of Hugh's discoveries and their importance.

'He was a remarkable man,' Ian added, gathering up his tools to go, 'remarkable.' I thought so too.

'We are currently doing a project on Hugh Miller,' my grandfather told Ian, who looked amused. 'Alice helping you then?' he asked politely.

'No' said my grandfather at exactly the same moment I said that yes, she was. Ian looked amused yet again. 'Well, I expect she is helpful. She's a helpful sort of a girl!' Alice just smiled that quiet smile that she has.

Of course Hugh wrote about the day he went to explore his theory about finding fossils on the beach at Cromarty that should have matched the ones at Eathie:

'The first nodule I laid open contained a bituminous-looking mass, in which I could trace a few pointed bones and a few minute scales. The next abounded in rhomboidal and finely-enamelled scales of much larger size and more distinct character. I wrought on with the eagerness of a discoverer entering for the first time a *terra incognita* of wonders. Almost every fragment of clay, every limestone nodule contained its organism - scales, spines, plates, bones, entire fish …'

But not one fossil did Hugh Miller find that matched those at Eathie, not one:

'I had got into a different world and among the remains of a different creation … I wrought on until the advancing tide came splashing over the nodules and a powerful August sun had risen toward the middle sky; and, were I to sum up all my happiest hours, the hour would not be forgotten in which I sat down on a rounded boulder of granite by the edge of the sea, when the last bed was covered, and spread out on the beach the spoils of the morning.'

Our project was coming along. We used the entries in the columns to make charts that we stuck up on the wall. I went most mornings to get photocopies and I did the lettering and writing up of small panels, mostly from *My Schools and Schoolmasters*, but sometimes from Hugh's other works and books that we found at the museum or at a shop in Cromarty called *The Emporium* that sold new and second-hand books and other things, and made a bit of a speciality of the local hero.

I spent an hour or two every day in the museum with my notebook until I felt like I really *knew* Hugh Miller. I almost expected him to come walking up the street to my grandfather's house. I would recognize him at once, of course, from his springy hair and wild mutton-chop sideburns. I would also recognize him from the shepherd's plaid he always wore, even when he became well known. It was his trademark — but I don't think he really needed one. He was famous for more things than just finding fossils, although he was known all over the world for that when he was older and had discovered some unknown kinds of fossil fishes. He corresponded with the great men of geology everywhere.

In the museum, I got a real sense of what his life had been like. The birthplace cottage, where he began his life, was very simple and quite dark with a very low door to stoop under into the house. The main museum was the house his father built before the ship went down. My favourite was the top floor where there was a lot about geology and where I saw the fossil fishes of the Old Red Sandstone, for which Hugh Miller became famous. One of them was named after him - *Pterichthyodes milleri*. I wondered what that must have felt like.

I could not imagine.

CHAPTER TEN

Alice surprised us the next day. She often does.

'I've brought my part of the project,' she announced. For an instant my grandfather's eyes flickered towards mine. 'Good!' he said a bit too heartily.

'Yes,' she went on. 'I thought it could go under the "person" column, since you don't have one for "husband" or even "boyfriend". I noticed for the first time that she had a roll of cardboard under her arm.

'Good …very good,' my grandfather said, rubbing his hands together, rather nervously, I thought.

Carefully, she slid two lilac rubber bands off the ends of her cardboard and then, with a quick sideways glance to see if we were watching properly, rolled it open.

She must have taken time over it. Most of the writing was done with a different coloured pen for each letter. That takes a long time. I know because I tried it once and gave up after the second word. Hugh Miller (the dreamy early calotype where he is looking down) dominated the left hand side. On the right was a picture I knew from the museum, one of a sweet, smiling young lady with dark ringlets and deep eyes. She was Lydia, the girl who changed Hugh's life yet again when he met her in Cromarty.

I knew I had to say something. My grandfather was noticeably silent. 'It's very … nice.' I managed. There was a flash of disappointment in her eyes, so I tried a bit harder.

'I like the way you have done the writing,' I told her. 'I tried it once, but it was too difficult. And this bit here,' I pointed to a part with hearts with flowers twined around them. 'Very … um, lovely.'

'Those flowers are called myrtle,' she explained. 'That was their special flower! He wrote a poem to her with it in. She even used it as her pen name when she wrote stories for children. Mrs Myrtle was her writer's name.'

I looked at my grandfather. No help there. I looked at Alice again. She looked … well she looked a bit like a kitten I was once offered by a boy beside the station in Canon Hills. Pleading. 'It's fabulous,' I said and suddenly I really meant it. 'Thank you … Alice.'

You would think I had given her a birthday present — a big one. My grandfather grinned. I took the cardboard and taped it carefully up on the wall between "person" and "writer". 'That looks right,' I said. 'Are you happy with that?'
'Yes,' Alice said, and I knew she was.

Lydia was another change in Hugh's life. He never mentions girls before he met her. I once asked my grandfather if that was normal and he said, quite crossly, yes, it *was* back then, in the days when people were not so completely daft and soppy. I wonder if Hugh had girlfriends, or if he was too busy with nodules and theories of the structure and history of the earth? There was no answer to that, nor ever would be, but he sure took a hit when he met Miss Lydia Fraser.

She was pretty — not in the way that Alice is, with her pale silvery looks, but pretty enough and clever too. She had read a lot of books and played the piano and did all the kinds of things that well brought up young ladies did in those days.

Hugh was busy being a monumental mason and chatting to people in the churchyard at Cromarty and other places while he carved memorial stones with a scalloped edge that was another of his trademarks. Lydia went to see him doing that and was very impressed, although he says he didn't notice her at the time.

He noticed her soon afterwards all right:

'... very pretty and, although in her nineteenth year at the time, her light and somewhat petite figure and the waxy clearness of her complexion, which somewhat resembled that of a fair child rather than a grown woman, made her look from two to three years younger. And as if in some degree a child, her two lady friends seemed to regard her. She stayed with them a scarce minute ere she tripped off again; nor did I observe that she favoured me with a single glance. But what else could be expected by an ungainly, dust-besprinkled mechanic in his shirt sleeves and with a leather apron before him?'

Maybe he *really* didn't notice her at first, and maybe that was because she was from a different part of the society of Hugh's time — the slightly upper bit. Maybe he didn't think it was worth bothering when they were so far apart in the general way of things. But Lydia did. She told him so later when they were what my grandfather called 'courting'. She had come especially to see what 'the poet of Cromarty' looked like, because by this time our Hugh had quite a reputation as a published poet (although he published his poems himself) and a writer in the newspapers. He wrote a piece about the herring industry that Sir Walter Scott himself wanted to read and Hugh Miller was highly thought of in the drawing rooms of Cromarty. They called him a literary lion and, I would think, there might have been quite a few young ladies wanting to see what he looked like.

It was not long before Hugh and Lydia were meeting for quiet walks in the woods behind Cromarty, reading to each other from books they had discovered and, I suppose, falling in love. Lydia's mother forbade an engagement at first, but gave in when she saw how things went. They could consider becoming engaged, she said, but only in three years — or before that if Hugh found a profession more suitable than that of mason — and when he was earning more money. Poor Hugh!

'Would you like to go for a walk?' Alice said suddenly into the silence.

Oh dear!

It was quite hot, so we drifted along the beach for a bit with our feet in the water at the edge of the beach, and then we turned towards the path up the South Sutor. It was a lazy kind of afternoon. It had been quite a hard week — and now there were only five more days before my mother arrived. I tried not to think about that. The project was in good shape and my grandfather had encouraged me to take an afternoon off. 'Fresh air will do you good,' he said, eyeing his Sunday newspaper and a bit of a late afternoon nap. It was a time for drifting, a time for thinking.

The caves still called to me. I often thought about them in that half-sleep, half-awake when you think your real thoughts. I told Alice.

'I've never been there,' she said. 'Let's go.'

So we went.

It wasn't quite like I had thought. Things seldom are. It wasn't as dramatic as I had expected, but then I knew the story. It was, I suppose, a bit like cheating and reading the ending of a book without bothering about the middle. We lay on our stomachs and peered over the edge. I never — not for a single instant — felt like jumping down, and neither did Alice. I *did* wonder if she would jump if I asked her, but it didn't seem fair, so I didn't. We just looked at the place where *they* had, and then went on to see if we could spot any dolphins coming in from the Moray Firth and talk about other things that, actually, had nothing at all to do with Hugh Miller.

At first Alice had been … well, I suppose I had mostly thought of her as a *girl*, just reading away in the background. I had never even asked her why she was doing that. I did now.
'Guide badge,' she said in her usual way. 'But I got to like doing it.'
Oh. Guide badge. What had I expected?

It was getting dark when we got back to my grandfather's house — and surprisingly dark there too. Where *was* he? He never went out at this time. Never. I looked at Alice - and she looked at me.

'The caves!' she breathed. 'He's gone to look for us! He thinks we went to the caves!'

Well, we *had* gone to the caves, but we were sensible enough not to have done anything daft. Didn't he know that? But I knew Alice was right. I knew that's where he had gone - I *knew* it.

It took hardly any time to run there, or maybe that's just what it felt like. What was the state of the tide? I had no idea. Would he just go there and call for us? Would he do anything ridiculous and heroic? Would he remember things he had done in the army and try to be brave? I had no way of telling, I just ran.

Luckily Alice had thought to grab his torch, because it was much darker when we got back to the edge of the cliff above the cave. A pale moon was rising, shining its watery light across the waves pounding in on the sand below. Low tide, I noticed. Wouldn't be able to get a boat in for a bit, not over those rocks. We stretched out on the springy turf again.

'Mr Ross? Mr Ross?' Alice called down. 'Are you there?' She shone the faint light of the torch downwards and my heart stopped. He *was* there! He was lying awkwardly against a rock and, I saw, in about the same position Hugh Miller and his friend had managed to put themselves in — stuck.

'Gramps!' I yelled at the top of my voice, and it seemed to bounce back at me, over and over again from the cliffs. '*Gramps! Gramps!* And then, after a few seconds, *Gramps! Gramps!*

Alice held the light on his face and, just for an instant his eyelids fluttered open and then closed again.

'Finally!' he said, and then spoke no more.

Appalled, I looked at Alice. She looked steadily back at me. 'Finally?' I said. 'What does finally mean?' She shook her head. She didn't know either. After that, it didn't seem to matter how much we called and shouted. He just lay there.

'We should get help,' Alice said gently. I knew that, but who would go? If I went, that would leave Alice here alone in the dark. If she went that would leave …

'I'll go,' Alice said. 'It will be better if you are here if … when … he wakes up.' I knew she was right, but it didn't feel good to let her go off like that. I watched her until she was out of sight down the path, her pale hair catching the gleam of light from the rising moon, the beam of the torch stretching ahead of her.

It was very dark after she had gone. I put my head down on the turf and felt tears begin to gather like hot wax behind my eyes. 'Gramps!' I said softly again. He must have heard me. There was a low moan. He was alive!

I wasn't sure what to do. Probably it was best to stay where I was, but then my grandfather was alone, down there. I thought about it. He groaned again. I slid myself over the edge. For a moment I just hung there, feeling the weight of my body over the space. Then I let go.

It was a mistake. I knew that even before I hit the ground and heard the sharp snap of something in my ankle. I certainly knew it when I found out how dark it was down there. I knew it even more when I felt around with my hand and found my grandfather's face. He made a spluttering sound.

'What the devil are *you* doing down here?' he asked crossly.

'I came to find out how you are,' I said. It sounded a bit weak, even in my own ears. 'To see if you are hurt — and to find out what "finally" means.' After a moment I added, 'I thought you were … dead.'

He snorted then, in that way he has, then sighed. 'I am not dead. I am alive. I have broken, I think, my ankle and cracked my head against a rock. I was unconscious for a brief amount of time, during which I distinctly heard somebody calling me "Gramps" so I expected it was you.' Then he added more quietly, 'you haven't called me that since you were little.'

I thought about that. I hadn't really called him anything, since I got here, and in my mind I always said 'my grandfather'.

'Sorry,' I said. He didn't answer. At least I knew what finally meant.

We lay there for a bit without saying anything more. It

wasn't uncomfortable and, after the first bit, my ankle didn't hurt too much.

'What damage did you do. When you jumped?' he asked after a while.

'I didn't jump. I slid gently off the ledge. It was just an accident that my ankle got caught.'

He snorted again. 'I didn't jump either. Bit of erosion when I leaned forwards to see if you were down there.' He gave a little laugh. 'Hugh Miller would have had an interest. Cliffs always eroding away. Sea taking the land, that sort of thing.' Then after another pause. 'Thanks. Better down here with company. Did young Alice go to get help?' I admitted that she had. 'Plucky one that. Good friend to have. She'll be all right.' I thought so too.

It was strange lying there with Gramps. The sky had become intensely black, like ink for dipping pens, and here and there were patches of stars. The moon had disappeared behind some cloud.

'I wonder what Hugh Miller would have said,' I asked more to make conversation in the silence than anything else, 'if he could have known what we do now?'

'What we know now? We know nothing!'

'Well … not nothing. We've been to the moon and …'

'We know *nothing*! I felt his arm move. He was pointing at the dark star-sky.

What do we know about *that*? He asked. His pointing finger travelled across the sky and seemed to stop. 'What do we know about *that* one?'
'Which one?'

He barked. 'You choose. What do we know about any of them? And then he picked up a handful of muck. 'Or this? What do we know about *this*, except that maybe that's where we came from.'

Then we just lay in silence, thinking about Hugh Miller, thinking about things.

CHAPTER ELEVEN

Alice arrived after about an hour with a whole crowd of people including several paramedics and a man with a notebook who wanted to know if it was a pact, or had we jumped separately. Gramps was quite cross about that. 'Damn fool,' he muttered under his breath. 'Course I didn't jump. It was natural causes! Erosion!'

They set up some lights and, after an interminable time, we were back on the top of the cliff. They took Gramps first and it was a strange feeling to watch the sling inch up the rock with Gramps in it, pale but focused.

When it was my turn, I realised how intensely tired I was. I *longed* for my bed in the small room under the eaves in my grandfather's house. My ankle was like a small fire at the end of my leg. My eyes kept wanting to close. We had to go to the clinic first, of course, and they decided to keep us in overnight. Which was reasonable, I suppose. Gramps had a fracture in his right ankle, I had a damaged tendon in my left ankle and we were both, apparently, suffering from shock and possibly mild exposure. I let them look after me. Somebody brought me hot cocoa and some Marmite toast. It was good. Then there were slippery-cool sheets and then there was sleep.

Mum was not best pleased when she was informed in the morning. They took the phone to Gramps and I heard him trying to tell her about the erosion and the natural causes. Then she asked to speak to me.

'Are you OK?' she asked, rather crisply, I thought.

'Yes, Mum.'

'I'll not be able to change my plans,' she said, still crisp. 'I'm coming up to Inverness by plane and I will hire a car at the airport. I'll be in Cromarty by five in the afternoon on Friday. We can discuss the future then.' My heart sank. 'And try to stay out of *trouble!*'

'But, Mum ...'

It was no use. She had put the phone down.

Hugh Miller fell into a bit of a dilemma when he fell in love with Lydia. He was thirty-five — ten years older than her — and he had no steady income, not much in the way of savings and no interest in being sponsored by somebody rich. It was not in his nature. He wanted to do things his way.

But he was offered a chance at something better when the local bank invited him to work there and be the accountant. I can't think of much worse, myself! He had to look after the bank's interests and make sure money was not lent to the wrong sort of person when the manager was away, balance the books every evening (without even a calculator!) and look after the actual money. He even bought a pair of large pistols for times when he had to take money to other places!

He also worked on the manuscript of his first book. It had a catchy title too; *Scenes and Legends of the north of Scotland; or the traditional History of Cromarty.* For this book he interviewed all the old grannies, grandpas and aunties he met, remembered the stories of his mother and wrote down many stories that would otherwise have been lost:

> 'I found it a new and untrodden field, full of those interesting vestiges of past time which are to be found – not in the broken remains of palaces and temples, but in the traditional recollections of the common people.'

The museum display reminded us that this idea was indeed a new one. Another 'ology' came into the picture as Hugh began to be intrigued by what came to be called Anthropology. Was there anything this man wasn't interested in?

Hugh Miller hardly wasted a second when he was awake. I struggle to get all the words down in this journal as well as the writing for the project. Hugh did a hundred times as much writing every day, after working in a bank with columns of figures and also dreaming around the woods a bit with Lydia in the evenings.

But working in the bank did mean that he could get married, and that was what he wanted more than anything. Well, to get married and live with Lydia — and look for fossils in his spare time. They were married by Hugh's good friend, the local minister Reverend Mr Stewart, and then enjoyed a honeymoon of a whole two days during which Hugh had important discussions (about fossils) with a friend in Elgin, where they went for the break.

Most of Hugh Miller's writing is complicated and serious. But sometimes he stands back a little bit from intellectual things. When that happens, you get a strong feeling of *being* there. When he writes about this time of his life, you know how happy he was. Maybe working at the bank was a bit boring, but — once he had managed to balance the figures for the day — there were the long summer evenings, or the long winter ones, spent with his wife and his fossils. Lydia wrote about this time:

'*He took pleasure when he could — for this was rare — in sitting with fossil shelves around him, and with a heap of literary confusion about, which was order to him, and which no hands might touch. And if I came in and sat on his knee and talked to him a little, that was his paradise. But of personal ambition, other than to write something which men would not willingly let die, he had not a single grain.*'

They lived in Miller House that is now the main museum. Hugh's fossils and books were kept where the geology display is now. I've stood there and imagined how it might have been — and sat in the music room where Lydia played to him on the piano (when she managed to lure him away from his fossils) and maybe sang to him the songs of Robert Burns that play now from a CD player in the cupboard. It makes me a bit sad.

In the evenings, in summer, Hugh and Lydia would sometimes go out in a small boat he had and catch fish for their supper. Maybe they took picnics with them. Maybe, just maybe, Hugh looked about a bit for fossils when they landed on small beaches. (Ha!). They were happy. Maybe when Hugh looked back on some of those happiest hours he spoke of in connection with nodules, he found that most of the others came from this quiet time, with Lydia, before change caught up with him again.

Gramps sometimes asks me: 'What have you learned? What have you *learned*, laddie?' Usually I tell him the facts I had learned (and there were a lot of them on the Hugh Miller project). Now I began to see that he meant to ask me what was I learning about life. *Schools and Schoolmasters* was about learning from life. It hadn't taken long to work that out — particularly with heavy pointers from Gramps and Hugh Miller himself. But what had I learned in these past few weeks, about life, my life?

When I came here, I was just angry. That was all, just that. Now, when I thought, like Hugh Miller, about the happiest hours, there were some, and they were here in Cromarty and I had enjoyed them. They had pushed out some of the bad hours, moved them down the conveyor belt of my mind, so they were not standing up at the front, jeering at me. Maybe that was what I was learning here? Maybe I was learning that you don't know when happiness is coming (or going) but you have to grab hold of it and enjoy it while it is there.

Hugh Miller and Lydia had a golden time in Cromarty after they were married. It didn't last very long. Their first child, a daughter they called Eliza, was born in 1837. She died of a fever before her second birthday.

Hugh was devastated. After a period of extreme grief and heartbreak, he took up the tools of his stonemason trade and made the headstone for the grave of his child — the one that I had seen myself in an old burial ground on the way towards the Sutors. Change was coming.

My mind-picture of Hugh had changed, over the weeks. In the beginning, he was a boy like me, running wild over the hills and beaches of Cromarty. Then I began to see him as a young man, striding around the Scottish countryside, testing out life with the rough bunch of masons, making contact with the real life of poor people at that time; knowing how hard it was.

Now he was a more solid figure, married, writing hard — serious work that was taken that way by intelligent and educated people in Edinburgh and even in other places in the world He seemed … bigger.

It occurred to me that, when his story began for me, he was able to play with ideas, play with life even. Gradually, as he got older, he moved from that into a harder place.

Gramps says that one part of Hugh's brilliance was his ability to be in both the world of the poor and downtrodden people of Scotland and — at the same time — write himself up to the intellectual end of society, including marrying Lydia.

I found that difficult to understand at first. Maybe now I began to. But it must have been hard. The project was nearly finished. I had heard and read an awful lot about Hugh Miller. I maybe knew more about him than I knew about anybody else (that was a thought). But did I know what he *felt* like? Did he tell us that? Maybe. Maybe those happy hours were what shone through all the other stuff and showed us what was the essence of Hugh Miller. Maybe that's why I found now, when I thought about it, that I liked him. I *liked* him a lot.

My grandfather peered over my shoulder at the cramped project columns. My handwriting seemed to be getting smaller and smaller as I tried to fit in more information. I stopped writing and looked up at him. He smiled.

'Why did he go to Edinburgh? I asked. 'Why didn't he just stay here, with Lydia — and his fossils — where he was happy?'

My grandfather sighed. 'He left because he was a man of conscience, a man of morals. He left because he was called to go and he could not ignore the call.' He sighed again. 'Hugh was a man of principle.'

I looked down at the columns. I thought about words like principle and courage and conscience and they seemed to blur before me as tears came into my eyes. I hoped my grandfather didn't see. I don't think he did, because he put his hand on my shoulder and went on talking about Hugh Miller.

'There was difficulty with the way the government in London was dealing with a dispute in the Scottish church. Hugh didn't agree with what was being done. He wrote a letter to Lord Brougham, in London, that really impressed people in Edinburgh who felt the same way. They were about to launch a newspaper — that was *The Witness* that we have looked at together in the museum — and they invited him to be its editor.'

'Sounds straightforward enough, I said, and my voice hardly shook.

'No,' my grandfather said softly. 'Nothing like that is ever straightforward. It meant a huge change for Hugh and Lydia and a move away from a place they loved. It was hard but they did it.' He paused for a moment. 'I'll just make us a wee cup of tea.' I heard the sound of him limping over to the kettle on his crutches.

It was just as well. A big, fat blob of water fell suddenly on the columns, and then another. Thinking about Hugh Miller's family made me think about my own, it made me remember. It made me remember my dad, and I tried never to do that.

I used to be so proud of him, when I was little. He was manager of our big local football club — I even saw him on television sometimes, pacing up and down when the team was doing badly and chewing gum and waving his arms about angrily.

That was before the scandal and the newspaper reports about the money that wasn't there and the players who hadn't been paid the big transfers they had been promised. That was before he got the girlfriend and walked out on Mum; walked out on me.

A picture came to my mind of my father at the special meeting they called about me at Canon Mills Comprehensive after …

after Georgie died, when the head teacher felt the need to haul my dad back from wherever he had been skulking.

'Mr Alexander,' he said. 'Are you prepared to stand up for your son, who has been accused by these boys here of lying and telling tales about bullying in this school? Bullying that, I might remind you, your son, and nobody else, claims to have caused the regrettable death of one of our pupils. Are you? He claims to have heard laughter — laughter that he claims he recognised. He has no evidence. Nobody else has come forward. I am asking you to answer for him. Should we investigate further?'

'No,' my father said softly, his eyes never leaving the floor, which he had been staring at fixedly for the whole time.

'Mr Alexander, these are serious allegations. Your son is unsupported in this. Do *you* support him in his stance? '

'No.' He flashed a look in my direction, a look of dislike. 'He's big enough now. He must stand up for himself. He's nothing to do with me.'

Later, when he passed me on the way out, my father scowled at me. 'Who do you think you are, stirring up trouble? Just keep your stupid mouth shut, like I told you.' He glared at me again. 'Just keep your stupid *mouth* shut!'

That was the last time I saw him.

That night I dreamed about Georgie Crawford. I wasn't allowed to have that dream. I didn't *allow* myself. When it happened, I woke myself up and just made myself think about something else. Sometimes it worked. But sometimes, like this night, it didn't.

It was real and it wasn't real somehow at the same time. Maybe I dreamed it? I wasn't supposed to be there. They'd seen me leave an hour before. They'd shouted some stuff — about my dad, mostly — and laughed, like they always did. But they had forgotten about me, and now I was back and they didn't expect me.

Georgie Crawford wasn't a special friend. I didn't have any special friends, or even any friends, really. But sometimes we hung out together. Sometimes we had fun. He was younger than me, but I liked him anyway.

I went back to get my maths assignment. If it had been anything else, I would have just left it. But it was for Mr Maggs. It didn't do to give Maggs ammunition.

In my dream, I was thinking about that as I came round the corner of the Science block and suddenly I wasn't. Suddenly my mind was filled with the sight of Georgie Crawford on the roof of the Sports store, on the middle bit where the roof pitches steeply away on both sides. He had both arms outstretched, like a tightrope walker. He was terrified.

His eyes held mine for an instant. His mouth moved as if he was going to say something … and then he lost his balance. For what seemed like an hour, he swayed. I held my breath. Then, with a small cry, he slipped. There was a thud where his body hit the corrugated iron, another as he hit the guttering and then a sickly smack as he hit the ground. The dream slowed down as I walked towards him; there was the sound of ghostly laughter — laughter I had heard many times. When I got to Georgie, he was dead.

He was dead in the real world too. I tried to tell them about the dream, and the laughing … they didn't believe me. They were kind, but they didn't believe me. They offered me counselling. They called Mum in Toronto and she said she would get back as soon as she could. I had a week off school. I kept trying to tell them about the bullying and the Malcolm Todd gang and the laughing. I kept trying to tell them — for Georgie — but it was too late for him, and nobody would listen.

They particularly wouldn't listen when I mentioned Malcolm's sidekick, the boy who egged him on all the time, Stephen Maggs.

Like father, like son. Stephen Maggs.

After that, I took my dad's advice. I didn't say anything. Georgie Crawford hadn't.

CHAPTER TWELVE

Eventually, it was Friday. We were pretty busy that week, Gramps and I, getting the cottage tidied up and sorting out the kitchen, but mostly with finishing the project. Gramps fretted about it. Had we missed anything important in Hugh Miller's Cromarty years? Had we made a mistake in not following through to Hugh and Lydia's life in Edinburgh, when he was called to edit *The Witness* and spent sixteen hard years doing his thousands of words a week? What about the summers, when he went with his old friend Reverend Mr Swanson on the leaking old boat that served as a floating manse and made geological discoveries in the west of Scotland? What about the family he and Lydia enjoyed with their four other children — and Lydia's career as a successful writer of children's books? What about all that?

In the end, it was all I could do to calm him down, not the other way round.

'Gramps!' I said as firmly as I could manage. 'The man wrote so much ... we can't hope to cover it all in a few weeks! We *agreed* it was just going to be the Cromarty years.' He nodded, but slowly. 'And anyway, we don't have time to go to Edinburgh and do proper research. It's a whole different project!

In the end he saw the logic in that. And time had run out on us in any case. The house sparkled like some kind of advertisement for house-cleaner. The walls of the sitting room were decorated with our posters. We'd even asked Gramp's friend, the lady from the museum, round for her approval and she had been very pleased.

'Gosh!' she had said. 'You *have* done a lot!'

Now we just waited for the sound of Mum's hire-car. Alice came round to offer moral support. When we heard the wheels on the bit of gravel that Gramps has for visitors' cars, we all looked at each other for a moment and sat up straighter.

My mother came in. She looked … anxious, as if she didn't know what to expect. For a moment she just looked, without saying anything. Suddenly I saw what she was seeing. Gramps in one armchair with his left foot in plaster and up on a stool. Me in the other armchair with my *right* foot in plaster and up on a stool. Alice sitting primly on a dining room chair with her hands folded in her lap and her silvery hair well brushed. A multitude of posters about Hugh Miller decorating all the walls and a pile of research books (and the Hugh Miller Series) on the table. She couldn't see the air, but it was full of tension and I expect she could feel it.

She kind of sagged against the doorframe. Nobody said anything after the initial hellos. We just looked at her — and she looked at us.

Then she began to laugh. It was a small laugh at first and then it grew into a bigger laugh. She laughed so hard that she began to cry and had to sit down.

'If you could just *see* yourselves!' she gasped. 'You look so ...' I was sure she was going to say "ridiculous" but she didn't '... so *worried*!' Then she cried a bit more and the sobs got out of control, like she was never going to stop. Gramps signalled to me that maybe Alice and I should slip away. So we did.

'Oh, Isobel,' I heard him saying, and his voice was soft. 'Oh, Isobel, why didn't you come to me? Maybe I could have helped.' Then we just heard the sound of mum crying, but this time it wasn't the awful crying from before; more like crying she needed to do, somewhere she was safe.

Alice and I sat in the sun, out of earshot. The sea was gently breathing. So was I.

'Did the school burn right down to the ground?' she asked suddenly. She must have been thinking about that quite a bit, I realised. I had never finished the story.

'No. The caretaker was walking his dog and he saw the fire begin. The fire engines came really quickly when he called them.' 'Oh,' she said. Alice is good at one-word sentences. 'And did you get punished?'

'No ....' I said. But she deserved to know more. 'There was an internal commission of inquiry about the fire. They said there were extenuating circumstances … they let me off with a warning.' I thought for a moment. 'There were people who didn't want … didn't want some things to come out. They said I had been under pressure since … well, for a long time. They …' But I couldn't speak any more about that terrible time. 'Mum sent me up here to get me away from all the … talk.'

Another person would have asked what the extenuating circumstances were. Alice didn't. So I told her anyway. It was the first time I had spoken the words.

'I had a friend … Georgie Crawford. He died. I did it for him.'

She did that thing again, she reached over and touched me, just with the one finger on my arm 'I'm sorry you lost your friend,' she said softly. 'But now you have another one.'

We just sat in silence in the sun after that, with our backs against the warm stone of the sea wall. But I knew this was one of the golden hours that I would always remember.

Gramps gave Mum my journal to read. We had agreed on that on our last night alone in front of the Carboniferous forest fire.

'You may not be able to *talk* about what happened,' Gramps said slowly. 'But you have written it, have you not?' He had watched me, but he had never asked before.

'Yes.' I said.

He sighed, a very deep sigh. 'Your mother has had a difficult time … a very difficult time.' He sighed again. 'Not as difficult as you, perhaps, but hard.' I did know that.

'I never liked that man … your father … the man she married but,' and he tipped his head on one side and looked at me, 'you may well find out that love does strange things to people.' Yeah. I had noticed that too.

Mum and I drove up to the top of the south Sutor to talk. We could look out over the sea and the yellow gorse on the opposite side and there were even (finally) dolphins playing and dancing down below.

It wasn't like on television, like in the soap operas where everything suddenly comes right. But we talked, and she hugged me, and I hugged her back, and I really meant it. At last I felt at home with my mother in a way I hadn't in the last year. And my father wasn't there in the car with us, not for a moment, not for a moment.

He was history.

POSTSCRIPT

Later that summer, when things had settled down a bit, Gramps and I got on with our reading. We didn't need a fire — sometimes it was even warm enough, and light enough, to sit outside in the evenings.

Mum was considering whether to move up to Cromarty again. 'There's the cottage over the way,' Gramps had said, 'where Jamie started his career on Hugh Miller.' He gave one of his little private smiles. 'It wouldn't take much fixing up. There's a very good secondary school at Fortrose, not far away. It would suit Jamie. Maybe you could think about that antique shop you always talked about when you were young? So Mum had gone back south to 'have a think' as she said. Change. I hoped she would do it. I hoped we would do it. I'd asked her if we could, on that last day, before she went back. She had smiled and said we mustn't rush into things - but I could see she was tempted.

Meanwhile there was the summer in Cromarty. Gramps was thinking about a trip to Edinburgh to see where Hugh Miller and his family lived when they were there. 'I particularly want you to see some of the dressed stone. It is important to realise how much of Edinburgh was built with the input of men like Hugh, who cut the stone.'

Uncle Ian was also making plans. These involved taking Alice (and me) to see some other fossil sites and help him, as he put it, with some of the heavy work.

I didn't think about the old things much, and I didn't think about Hugh Miller as much either. But there was one thing that caught my eye and stayed in my mind. Something that Hugh wrote when he was geologizing in Orkney. Something that maybe summed up what did go on in his head when he was out looking for fossils and thinking. It was in a book called *Rambles of a Geologist*, which was published with the book he wrote about the floating manse where he spent summers with his friend. That one was called *The Cruise of the Betsy* and was my favourite of all the books.

Hugh was caught in a storm and took shelter in a stone tomb, a mysterious and lonely place on the island of Hoy, on Orkney, full of mysteries and stories and dreams. This is what he wrote:

' ... I found (the rock) lettered over with the names of visitors; but the stone, - an exceedingly compact red sandstone, — had resisted the imperfect tools at the command of the traveller, — usually a nail or knife; and so there were but two names decipherable, — that of an "H. Ross, 1735," and that of a "P. FOLSTER 1830." The rain still pattered heavily overhead; and with my geological chisel and hammer I did, to beguile the time, what I very rarely do, — added my name to the others, in characters which, if both they and the Dwarfie Stone get but fair play, will be distinctly legible two centuries hence. In what state will the world then exist, or what sort of ideas will fill the head of the man who, when the rock has well nigh yielded up its charge, will decipher the name for the last time, and inquire, mayhap, regarding the individual whom it now designates, as I did this morning, when I asked, "Who was this H. Ross, and who this P. Folster?"

I could visit the Dwarfie Stone. Orkney isn't that difficult to get to. I could save up. But I wish I could have gone there with Hugh Miller.

Imagine if I had done that all those two hundred and more years ago. There would be *our* names, carved in stone and people would say today ... who this Jamie Alexander, and who this HUGH MILLER?

AFTERWORD

The author of this book, Lesley Beake, was born and had her early schooling in Edinburgh, but has lived in South Africa ever since where she has established an enviable reputation as an editor and a writer of books for children with an African background, many of which have been translated into a variety of languages.

A couple of years ago one of the nieces of my late wife (great-great-granddaughter of Hugh Miller) suggested to me that although many young visitors to the Hugh Miller Museum in Cromarty showed great interest in it, we really needed a book for their age group which would introduce them to his life and writings and so encourage them to learn more about him than could be gained just from a visit to the museum. I was shown some books written by Lesley Beake, a friend of one of my wife's nephews, and immediately realised that she would be the ideal person to write such a book. She accepted my suggestion that I should commission her to do so and this, her 80th book, is the result. Being the professional she is she devoted months to background reading and research into the subject, about which she then knew nothing, and visited Cromarty to get a feel for the atmosphere and background. I believe Hugh Miller himself would share my view that she has proved truly worthy of the challenge.

In memory of my wife I am donating to Scottish charities that part of the proceeds from the sale of this book to which I would normally be entitled as owner of the intellectual property rights.

Henry McKenzie Johnston

ACKNOWLEDGEMENTS

Henry McKenzie Johnston
Reay Clarke
Hugh Clarke and Mary Cadogan
Janey Clarke
Dr Michael Taylor
Professor Nigel Trewin
Martin & Frieda Gostwick
James Robertson
Miranda and Henry Kitchen
The Friends of Hugh Miller

Illustrations by Jennifer Taggart

Book designed by Adam & Caron Kulesza
(Adam is the great, great, great, great grandson of Hugh Miller).
www.foliobespoke.com

If you want to know more about Hugh Miller, pay a visit to Cromarty and experience Hugh's birthplace for yourself. The museum is excellent. (It is, of course, completely illegal to carve names on, or otherwise deface, historical monuments.)

www.hughmiller.org – *an excellent website by Martin and Frieda Gostwick*

www.scran.ac.uk – *an invaluable source of information*

www.scottishgeology.com – *for some idea of the awe-inspiring geology of Scotland*

For further information on Lesley Beake: www.lesleybeake.co.za